Hudson sighed and rose to his feet with surprising speed as Seth saw the man to his right uncoiling like a sidewinder at the same time, and timing, damn it, was nine-tenths of any quick-draw contest!

Because Seth knew that was what it was. Real gunfighters never hemmed and hawed like kids in a schoolyard before they went for their guns. So Seth went for his Schofield as he crawfished back from the light, sickly certain this was it, for though it all seemed to be happening at the slow pace of a bad dream, his gun, and their guns, were on their way out and up through the thick air, and there was just no way he could aim at both, and Jesus which one should he be aiming at right now when both were throwing down at him and . . .

Also by Lou Cameron:

THE HOT CAR
THE SPIRIT HORSES
STRINGER
STRINGER ON ASSASSIN'S TRAIL
STRINGER ON DEAD MAN'S RANGE
THE GRASS OF GOODNIGHT*
THE BUNTLINE SPECIAL*
CROOKED LANCE*

Published by Fawcett Books

YELLOW IRON

Lou Cameron

FAWCETT GOLD MEDAL • NEW YORK

A Fawcett Gold Medal Book
Published by Ballantine Books
Copyright © 1990 by Lou Cameron

Library of Congress Catalog Card Number: 89-91544

ISBN 0-449-14599-9

Manufactured in the United States of America

First Edition: April 1990

DEMING, NEW MEXICO TERRITORY, 1886

General Nelson A. Miles felt he had enough on his plate with the Chiricahua out and the wires down somewhere between Deming and Lordsburg. So pending further notice all civilians were advised further travel east or west through the rugged hills of Apacheria would be at one's own damned-fool risk.

Seth Grant found the Jehu and shotgun messenger of the stage he'd boarded at El Paso taking such advice to heart indeed when he finally caught up with them in the Eagle Canteen that afternoon.

It hadn't been easy. He felt sure they'd been trying to avoid him and the other passengers. He knew he was right when the Jehu spotted him in the looking glass behind the bar, nudged his segundo, and turned to brazen it out with a casual hand resting on the grips of a Starr .36 and the smile of a bird dog that just didn't feel like getting wet again no matter what anyone said.

The thirty-year-old Jehu was a hard-cased cuss who'd killed more than one white man and knew it showed. He

1

knew his much younger and smoother-shaven passenger had just come west after growing up on a dairy farm in Essex County, New Jersey.

That might not have shown nearly as much as the Jehu felt it did had Seth Grant been a lying man, at all ashamed of who he might be and where he might hail from. East or west, blue denim jackets and jeans weathered much the same in the sun and wind, and Seth wore his old army-issue Schofield S&W neither prissy-high nor showboat low on his lean right hip. His new Stetson hat, Seth's only conscious attempt to blend in with his new surroundings, covered most of his short-cropped sandy hair and served to shade his day-old stubble and pleasant but nondescript features.

Just a tad above average height in his practical, stove-pipe boots, Seth was used to being taken for a typical country boy at first glance. It didn't bother him. He knew most gals were willing to dance with him at second glance and that few men with a lick of sense wanted to mess with him once they'd riled him enough to narrow his wide-set gray eyes and set his Celtic jaw. He'd come in here ready for peace or war. So he was still smiling as the Jehu said, "I know what you must be thinking, pilgrim. The gals in this town are snooty even when they don't get to charge as much. But what do you expect us to do about it?"

The stranded Seth Grant replied with neither bluster nor hesitation, "We all read the War Department notice they tacked up out front of the post office. It ain't for anyone but you to say whether you push on to Tombstone or not. But that was where I was headed, as you may recall me saying when I changed to your Butterfield Line."

The Jehu shrugged and said, "You can blame Naiche, Geronimo, or both, if the trace over Hatchet Pass ain't as safe as it used to be when you and me was young, Nelly."

Grant nodded and said, "I do. I can't say I've ever

heard of that other one, but Geronimo's even famous back east these days. Meanwhile, I hope you recall the matter being mentioned when we all boarded your Concord back there in El Paso and how you said we'd get refunds on the fares you collected there in advance.''

The Jehu snorted incredulously and replied, ''I did get you *most* of the way to Tombstone, didn't I?''

To which Grant could only morosely reply, ''I figure we're at least two hundred miles short, and to tell the pure truth I budgeted the long trip out here mighty tight. I'm down to pocket change and, at that, I'm still in better shape than that young Widow Baxter and her little boy.''

The Jehu seemed sincerely puzzled as he asked what that drab Baxter girl and her runny-nosed and whinesome kid had to do with this discussion.

Seth Grant smiled thinly and replied, ''I left them and my baggage on the veranda of the hotel just down the way. I bought 'em a penny licorice whip to share for lunch and said I'd bring their refund back with me. She was too proud to let me buy 'em the nickel sandwich I offered. But given the wherewithal to wire her kin in Tombstone, they ought to make it through the emergency. So let's see, at, say, a nickel a mile and make it a flat two hundred miles, we've each got . . .''

''Nada!'' The Jehu cut in, insisting, ''I turned the money in for safekeeping when we changed mules at Portrillo Wells, see?''

Seth Grant asked quietly, ''Now why would anyone have wanted to do that? You could have left the money in any number of banks at El Paso, and there's a swell bank right across the street, here in this county seat. Why on earth would anyone leave all our fares with a doubtless sweet old Mexican in the middle of that dry and dusty desert we just crossed?''

So there it was, buzzing in the smoke-filled air between

them like a sidewinder waking up in the greasewood. Folk at the bar gave them room as the Jehu purred to his segundo, "Did you hear that, Waco? I could swear someone just intimated this child was a liar! What did it sound like where you was standing?"

There was no answer. The shotgun messenger had wandered off somewhere quieter about the time the barkeep had taken down the looking glass and sent one of his swampers to fetch the law.

The Jehu said, "Look, kid, a man would have to be a fool to fight for an ugly gal and small change, right?"

Seth Grant nodded but said, "Plain-featured ladies need gents to stand up for 'em at least as much as pretty ones might. As to the fair price for a fight, I'd say that depends a heap on just how much one has left to eat on. As of now I've less than two whole dollars to get me two whole hundred miles. So don't try to tell me you ain't got it, and I won't have to say mean things about your word as a man."

Someone well out of either man's field of fire murmured, "Oh, Jesus, here we go!" but the Jehu favored Grant with a surprisingly boyish grin and declared, "Aw, hell, I ain't about to risk my job or worse for a few lousy bucks." And then he taught the youth from New Jersey one of the finer points of his western code by reaching for his six-gun instead of his wallet!

It almost worked. The Jehu was fast as well as treacherous. But to his numb dismay, in the time he had left to feel anything, the youth he had down as a callow farm boy got that .44 out faster and, more importantly, fired accurately as well as first.

Grant's round took the would-be gunslick over the heart to bounce him back against the bar, and from there he fell face-forward to the sawdust-covered floor. In the ringing silence that followed it occurred to Seth Grant that he hadn't been breathing for a spell. He managed not to let it show when he inhaled and marveled at how swell it felt to be able to do that, knowing you were still alive, after all.

Then the town law grumped in, sporting a gray handlebar mustache that almost matched the pewter mail-order badge pinned to the front of his gray hickory shirt. He had his old Walker conversion out and naturally pointed it at Seth Grant until a townsman he knew called out, "It was fair, Pecos. The one on the floor slapped leather first with results you can see for yourself."

The barkeep chimed in, "Said he was fixing to hand over some dinero. Went for his gun instead. Thought this other old boy, here, was a gone goose."

"Moves like spit on a hot stove," chimed in a less notable drunk, as the old lawman strode over to the body and Grant, unsure of the exact form, gingerly holstered his own six-gun.

There came a chorus of agreement to the effect that Seth was at least as quick on the draw as the late Henry McCarthy, William Bonney, Kid Antrim, Billy the Kid, or whoever in thunder the rascal had been afore Pat Garrett gunned him, dirty. The old lawman rolled the dead man over with one booted toe, took note of the sawdust and saliva-coated features, and muttered, "Oh, it's that surly Texas teamster again, or make that at last. I always figured someone would clean his plow if he kept at it."

The gent on familiar terms with old Pecos joined him above the sprawled cadaver to volunteer, "As I got the story, just listening in, the Jehu owed this Jersey boy and some lady money." Then the helpful cuss hunkered down without asking to haul out the dead man's wallet. When the town law made no objection he simply removed a couple of twenty-dollar silver certificates and waved them at the bemused winner of the shoot-out, observing, "This seems about right for the refunds you two was arguing about. What's left ought to bury the rascal decent enough, should neither kith nor kin come forward to carry his cadaver home to Texas.''

Seth Grant was no fool. He got over there and took the money before anyone could tell him not to. As he was putting it away the town law asked the helpful ghoul if there was enough left for, say, a more modest funeral and a few rounds of drinks in memory of the otherwise useless son of a bitch.

Amid the laughter that ensued the old-timer took Grant aside by one arm to tell him in a fatherly way, ''The county coroner's likely to want a written deposition from you afore you ride on, old son. You wasn't planning on leaving town tonight, I hope?''

Grant laughed weakly and replied, ''As a matter of fact, I was, but I don't see how I'll ever be able to push on to Tombstone until the army rounds up those Apache betwixt hither and yon, do you?''

The old timer shook his head cheerfully and said, ''Not hardly. Lucky for me I don't have to get through them Hatchet Hills in the near or distant future. For the army's been trying to keep them pesky Chiricahua rounded up for many a year, to no avail worth mention.''

The Luna County coroner's jury convened in the Grange Hall after sundown so everyone could enjoy supper and settle his innards a mite before getting down to more tedious chores.

Seth Grant was glad he'd put on his tan poplin travel duster as the sun was going down. For despite the early summer sun glaring a mite hotter out here in New Mexico, nights were way cooler than back home along the Third River.

He'd had to leave his gladstone grips in the safekeeping of the Eagle Canteen after the odd way Widow Baxter had behaved when he'd returned to her and her boy with their refund. He felt sure he'd never understand womankind if he lived to be a hundred, as he tried to put aside the way the fool gal had run off, beet-red, after letting her damned brat kick their savior in the shins and warn him to, "Leave my momma alone!"

Some of the others filing in had been present at the shoot-out that afternoon, but most hadn't. As Seth could best figure the form, he was supposed to take a seat on one side of the long trestle table they'd set up in the middle of the dance floor. So he did, as the other gents settled down on the far side to watch him, stare at their cigar tips, or, as in the case of one old gent in a rusty black suit, fall asleep right off aboard a folding chair.

Once they'd all settled down the details of the shoot-out in the Eagle Canteen didn't seem to interest the panel nearly as much as the doubtless exotic past of Seth Grant himself. The young easterner smiled sheepishly and said, "I've nothing to hide. But if the story of my life so far had been all that interesting, I'd have never come all the way out here in hopes of making it more interesting."

He reached under his duster for a cheroot to smoke in self-defense as he continued. "My dad fell at Cold Harbor, fighting for the Union. So I was raised on my maternal grandfather's farm betwixt the Hudson and the Wachung Mountains. We produced butter, eggs and truck, along with some fruit, and I don't mind saying that much work has to be better for one's character than his bank account. So when a sort of uncle wrote he'd landed a job in a silver mine out in Tombstone . . ."

"How can anyone have a *sort* of uncle?" a panel member cut in. Another next to him opened his own eyes wider and observed, "By Judas, he's right. An uncle has to be the brother of one's mother or father. That's the only sort of uncle there is."

Seth Grant lit his cheroot and pocketed the spent match as he explained, "Uncle Bob's on my late father's side, and to tell the truth he's never gotten along too well with my mother's side."

The juror who seemed to care nodded and said, "I had a black sheep uncle one time. He died with his boots on dealing faro in Fort Worth. Tell us how you learned to handle a six-gun so good on a dairy farm in Jersey state."

Seth smiled thinly and replied, "We were less than a day's ride out of Paterson, New Jersey, where Mr. Sam Colt first put together his wondrous machine."

A younger panel member sitting under a ten-gallon hat laughed knowingly and pointed out, "That well may be, but packing the same sort of gun Jesse James wore to herd *milk* cows . . . ?"

Seth Grant felt his ears turning pink. He said, "I hadn't heard you boys out here shot it out with your doubtless tougher *beef* cows. I'll confess shooting more at tin cans and such if you'll confess making love more often to your fist than anything prettier!"

This naturally brought the offended stockman to his feet with a threat to fill his fist with something more ominous. But the foreman banged the table with the butt of his own revolver, told them they were both out of line, and added, "I for one don't give squat whether this young gent winds up mining silver or milking cows. We've agreed the cuss he shot this afternoon had it coming, so let's nail it down as justifiable, and we'll have time for at least a couple of rounds on the way home, with the womenfolk none the wiser."

The ten-gallon wearer who'd been threatening another shoot-out for them to fret about seconded the motion. The motion was carried, and the foreman woke up the old vet they had down as the official coroner to tell him the hearing was over and he could go home and go back to sleep right. Seth Grant got to his own feet. But as he turned away from the trestle a burly, dark-featured juror who'd taken no part in the proceedings took him aside to say pleasantly, "They call me Elmo Dawson, and if mining is your pleasure, I'm your man. So we'd best have a talk about your future, pard."

Seth smiled thinly and replied, "I don't know beans about mining, and I can't say much for my future unless the army rounds those fool Indians up before the little money I have runs out."

Dawson nodded and said, "I gathered from your vague words about a silver-mining uncle that you didn't quite grasp the grim facts of hardstock mining. Follow me. There's some side steps we can sit on, private, whilst I fill you in on a few facts of life out our way."

With less than twenty-two dollars to last him Lord knew how long, Seth had no better place to go. Old Elmo didn't strike him as a gent who liked other gents in the Biblical sense, and they'd have hardly invited a stickup man to sit on their coroner's jury. So he went out that side door with the cuss and, sure enough, they wound up seated on some moonlit wooden steps with nary another soul in sight.

When Seth said as much Elmo Dawson chuckled and confided, "If you'd just hesh about Jersey state and allow you were from somewhere like West-by-God Virginia, nobody would argue. No offense, but you sure talk country, considering."

Seth asked innocently, "Considering what? There was nothing but country for miles around, no matter which way you spit over my grandad's fence. Of course, you have to get up around Ringwood or Mahwah to spy real New Jersey hill folk. Our Ramapos are a sort of spur of the Northern Appalachians and, I dunno, there must be something in the water up in all them wooded glens, for they tell me you get wild-eyed folk with extra toes and fingers in the Southern Appalachians as well.''

Elmo Dawson got out two expensive claro cigars. He said he was sorry he'd asked and inquired instead how well the young easterner might be able to ride.

Seth accepted the cigar with a nod of thanks but put it in his shirt pocket for later as he went on smoking his much cheaper cheroot. He said, ''I sit a horse well as most. We lived too far from any town worth mention for me to get there afoot of a Saturday night. Used to do some riding up and over the Wachungs as well. The hunting in our famous Great Swamp is swell, but you got to get there first.''

Dawson nodded, struck a match, and got his claro going before he decided. ''You'll do. I'm more in the market for a hand who's handy with a gun than any other kind. You see, Seth, I'm mounting me an expedition into the Hatchets, and at times like these there's no such thing as too many gun hands in and about Apacheria.''

Seth blinked incredulously and demanded, ''Hold on; are you even suggesting this would be a good time to go prospecting in Apache country?''

Dawson chuckled dryly and replied, ''There's never been a good time to *prospect* in Apacheria. Nobody with the brains of a gnat wants to be staring down at the ground when he ought to be keeping a sharp eye on the skyline all about him. On the other hand, since your uncle's enticed you to Tombstone on the far side of Apacheria, you doubtless know how old Ed Schieffelin found a swamping silver lode instead of his tombstone in the Dragoon Mountains, right?''

Seth shifted his weight sheepishly and allowed he'd never heard the story. Dawson said, ''All that's important to the here and now of it is that Schieffelin never made his strike by prospecting the fool rocks whilst Apache was on the prowl. He stumbled over the bones of two unknown prospectors who *had* been collecting ore samples whilst the runty red devils was creeping up on 'em.''

Dawson took another drag on his claro before he explained, ''The Apache neither torture nor pay much attention to unrefined ore. Schieffelin knew right off what it was he found scattered about with their dead bones. So he simply backtracked their trail to where they'd found it, and after him and his brother staked their own claims to the high grade, the rest was history. How do you like it so far?''

Seth smiled uncertainly and asked, ''Are you planning to scout for skeletons in those hills the sun just set behind?''

Dawson chuckled and replied, ''We can do way better than that. The strike's already been made and proven. Furthermore, it's gold, not silver, we're on our way to stake and claim. You see, this ain't the first time the Apache have riz. The last time they came out was a real pisser. If there's anyone Apache hate worse than us, it's Mexicans. So you can imagine what happened when the bands of Chihuahua, Loco, Mangas, Naiche and Geronimo all busted loose at once!''

Seth frowned uncertainly and said, ''Not really. Folk keep telling me Apache are *out*, or *loose*, this summer. Where are they supposed to be when they're not running wild betwixt the Dragoons of Arizona and the Hatchets of New Mexico?''

''On the swell reserves we've provided 'em, of course,'' replied the more knowledgeable westerner, adding, ''Naiche and Geronimo just jumped the San Carlos Agency, by themselves, so far, thank God. But never mind all that. My point is that Chief Loco and some of his braves hit this Mex mining camp a few days ride to the southwest and, well, they called him Loco because he

seemed a mite emotional, even by Apache standards. So
the greasers who weren't killed right out soon wished they
had been, and that was the end of their mining venture.''

''But their mine would still be there?'' asked Seth, who
wasn't too surprised to hear Dawson answer soberly,
''Their mine would still be there. Apache being supersti-
tious about even natural caves, I doubt they even peeked
into the mine. My plan is to simply tidy up what may need
to be tidied up, gather a little high-grade for the assay
office, and claim the abandoned mine for my own self. I
already have a guide and some other gun hands lined up.
I'd like to head up into the hills Saturday night, Geronimo
being a Christian convert who keeps the Sabbath and might
not have too many scouts out as we wend our way over
the first dozen hogback ridges.''

Seth smiled incredulously and asked, ''How good a
Christian might that other one, Naiche, be?''

Dawson shrugged and said, ''I don't know. Maybe
Benny does. It's a good point, and I mean to ask him as
we head out. I can pay you a dollar a day and found. You'll
naturally be riding my stock and packing my long-gun as
well as eating my beans. So what say you to the venture,
pilgrim?''

Seth studied the glowing tip of his cheroot as he replied
thoughtfully, ''I doubt I could make that much digging
post holes around here. But who's this Benny who knows
so much about Apache?''

Dawson explained, ''His real name sounds more like
Bay-nay-hay and he knows about Apache because he *is*
Apache. He was riding with Loco when they hit that gold
camp. So naturally he knows where it is. My plan is to
map and claim it formal whilst nobody else but us, the
army, and the wild ones are anywhere's near, see?''

Seth dropped his smoked-down cheroot between his
boots and stomped it out with a chuckle, saying, ''I ad-

mire a man who can get that drunk on cigar smoke. It appeals to the Scotch blood in me. Do you really expect anyone half-sober to follow an Apache up into Apache-infested hills for a buck a day and beans?''

Dawson soothed, ''Old Benny ain't on the warpath this summer. I told you he used to ride with Loco's band. He don't owe squat to any other chief and, unlike most of his kind, he's commenced to savvy the value of gold, or yellow iron as his kind calls it.''

Seth shook his head and said, ''I value my own skinny rump even more, and if I wanted Indians pegging arrows at it for pay, I'd up and enlist in the U.S. Cavalry.''

Dawson sniffed disdainfully and replied, ''Not at no dollar a day you wouldn't. The War Department pays thirteen dollars a month, and you get to dodge more than arrows. The left hand knoweth not what the right hand is up to at the Bureau of Indian Affairs. So most Apache pack repeating rifles these days.''

Seth got to his feet, muttering, ''You've convinced me, Elmo. I'd best just get a job here in town until this Indian trouble blows over.''

''Doing what?'' demanded Dawson, rising to his own feet. ''This is cattle and mining country,'' he pointed out. ''Unless you know how to rope as well as milk a cow you'll have a time hiring on at any spread in this neck of the woods, and I just offered you the only job with a mining outfit that figures to be open for a spell.''

He saw Seth was hesitant to burn bridges either way and added in a desperately casual tone, ''Of course, you might not last until you're really hurting for a job. As you told your tale inside, the sidekick of that Jehu you gunned got away, shotgun and all. Whether he means to be sensible about it or not, the man you just killed must have had at least a few friends driving for an outfit as big as Butterfield, and . . .''

"You said we'll be leaving Saturday night?" Seth cut in with a fatalistic sigh, to which Dawson replied more cheerfully, "I did, and you can bed down with us tonight, seeing you've no place half as safe to be right now."

As the youngest member of the outfit and an easterner as well, Seth Grant had been set for a certain amount of joshing. But he'd grown mighty weary of western attempts at wit by the time they rode out of Deming into a blood-red sunset. Elmo Dawson had introduced him to the one Indian and half-dozen white boys, none of them ten years older than him, by his given name. But after some even sillier experiments the ever-grinning Hamp Ferris, self-appointed second-in-command, had come up with Jersey Lilly and, naturally, that had stuck. They'd already had a "Kid" in the outfit in the person of Kid Wagner from Cheyenne, and at that Seth felt he might be a tad ahead of Virgin Joe from, naturally, Virginia City.

Rustic humor tended to be neither subtle nor gentle. The taller of the two pals who dipped snuff was called Big Dipper to distinguish him from who else but Little Dipper. The nickname Seth found unkindest of all was Pinto, for the chubby hand hired to rustle the grub. Pinto had a port-wine birthmark that made his fat face sort of jarring to gaze upon until one got used to it. But when Seth had asked the disfigured cuss what his real name might have been, old Pinto just clouded up and threatened to rain all over him. So there was nothing Seth could do but call him Pinto, too. The spotty-faced rascal wasn't much of a cook, either. But Seth knew it wasn't for him to say who tagged along or not.

The semi-domesticated old Apache Dawson had signed on got to be called something halfway closer to his real name, whatever Bay-nay-hay meant. It seemed doubt-some anyone would want to tease old Benny in any case.

In his Basque shirt of purple velveteen and crimson head-
band, old Benny might have passed for a mighty ugly
Mexican lady from the waist up. But below the hem of his
hip-length shirt his stocky brown legs ran down jay-naked
to the odd high-button moccasins his nation wore. At the
moment the old Indian was riding abreast with their boss,
old Elmo. Seth kept the buckskin barb he'd been issued
just behind their almost-matched bays. He couldn't make
out much of the country they were riding through, all with
carbines cocked across their thighs. He was hoping to pick
up helpful hints on survival from the one member of the
expedition who surely knew. But although Elmo Dawson
commented on this or that as they rode past, old Benny
just answered in soft sounds too gentle to qualify as grunts.
The few times Seth had heard the old Indian speak he'd
been struck by the high pitch and almost girlish tone of
the guide's odd accent.

The sun was down behind the jagged inky peaks ahead,
but the sky was still bright and the tips of the chaparral to
either side of the wagon trace still glimmered like old gold
in the gloaming. The Apache raised his right hand, Winchester and all, to rein in his pony and declare in that
almost sissy way, "Hear me, this is snake time, and we
don't know these horses well yet. Better we take break
now. Make coffee. Drink coffee. Give little crawling
brothers time to eat plenty rats and go back to dreaming
under bushes."

To his own mild astonishment Seth Grant understood.
So when Hamp Ferris bulled forward to complain that
they weren't five miles out of town yet, it was Seth who
told him, "I think we ought to listen to Benny here about
snakes at sunset, if this brushy country is heavy with
snakes as he says. Back home the best time to get struck
by a copperhead or diamondback was when it first commenced to cool after a hot, dry day. Snakes can't take

much baking. So they stay in the shade most of the day
and come out about now to hunt rabbits, rats, and such.
They don't like cold much more though. So as soon as
it really cools off they curl up some more someplace
and . . ."

"Did I ask you for a lecture on temperance, tobacco,
or a tinker's dam?" the huskier-built Hamp cut in. Seth
was saved from having to reply when Elmo Dawson declared indifferently, "We've at least as many snakes out
here as they might in New Jersey, and it was Benny here
as made the suggestion to begin with." Then he stood in
his stirrups to call back, "Pinto? We've time for coffee
and maybe cold cheese and hardtack, so get to it, and let
Virgin help you."

Virgin Joe called back, "Why me?"

"Because I said so. Build the fire on the trace, and
make it a small one. Watch where you put your big feet
as you traipse about for firewood. Did I want any of you
boys fanged by a sidewinder, we wouldn't be taking this
infernal trail break."

Seth Grant dismounted amid the general round of cat-
calls and cussing. He meant to make himself useful as
soon as he took care of his pony and took a leak. But first
things coming first he tethered the reins of his barb to what
he hoped was a mesquite bush and uncinched his heavy
Mex saddle as well. As he was carefully laying the saddle
on one side to dry the parts that usually went nearest the
horse, the old Indian passed, Winchester cradled over one
arm as his unreadable sloe eyes swept further out into the
gathering darkness. Seth cleared his throat and said, "Excuse me, ah, Benny. Could you tell me sure this was a
mesquite bush I tied this pony to?"

The Indian cast a casual eye at the suspect specimen of
local flora, and told Seth, "It is mesquite. Your horse can
eat those pods and even browse the leaves if it's careful

about the thorns. Next time don't try to stand up for me when my words are good enough to stand by themselves."

Seth flushed and protested, "Jesus H. Christ, I wasn't looking for an argument with nobody!"

The Apache nodded almost, and replied, "I know what was in your heart. I see you have unsaddled your horse even though we are only going to be here a short time. You still talk too much. Take care of your horse. Keep your guns clean and make sure they are always loaded when you are not cleaning them. Let other men fight with other men. Hear me, life is short enough, even if nobody kills you."

Seth nodded soberly, and said he'd try to keep such fine advice in mind. But he couldn't help asking if such observations on the average human life span had anything to do with Benny's somewhat calmer attitude these days.

The old Indian almost smiled despite himself, and replied, "I just told you it was best to let other men fight other men. I know Nelson Miles. I know Goyalka, the one you people call Geronimo. They are both too stupid to call men. Naiche is not as dumb. Nobody could be. But Naiche is the son of Cochise, and it bothers him that you white eyes are not as afraid of him as you were of his father. I understand what is in his heart. But hear me, I fight nobody, not even Nelson Miles, unless my own band comes out for another good fight. I don't think they will have a good fight this summer. I think a lot of people on both sides will die. Do as I just told you and maybe you won't be one of them. I have spoken."

As if to prove he meant what he said, the older man turned away and headed for the fire Pinto had just started further back along the wagon trace. Seth shrugged, watched where he was stepping, and relieved himself on the far side of the mesquite he'd tethered the barb to.

As he headed for the fire himself he found his path

blocked by Hamp Ferris. The somewhat older and much bigger man said, "I got me a bone to pick with you, Jersey Lilly."

Seth sighed, and said, "I was just discussing that with another wild westerner. If I was out of line I meant no harm, and you have my sincere and humble apologies. Can we drop it now, damn it?"

The husky Ferris seemed to need some time to think that over. As Seth tried to step around him the husky Hamp moved to block him again, and growled, "Not so fast, Jersey Lilly. You forgot to say pretty please, with sugar on it."

Seth sighed again, and said, "You remind me of this old boy back home. I think I was in the fifth or sixth grade. They had us all in the same one-room schoolhouse, with the big and little kids all mixed up. So Walter Howard, or Howard the Coward as we wound up calling him, must have been quite a bit older, as well as a head taller than me, and . . ."

"How come he let you call him Howard the Coward if he was bigger than you?" the bigger Hamp Ferris cut in with a puzzled scowl.

Seth smiled thinly and replied, "I had to whup him, chase him out of the schoolyard, and make sure he never came back until he'd allowed in front of the girls that he was scared to fight me before anyone called him Howard the Coward; and even then most of the smaller boys never called him that to his face."

Hamp Ferris drew himself up to an even more ominous height to demand, "Are you even hinting I'm afraid of you, Jersey Lilly?"

Seth smiled at him pleasantly to reply, "I surely hope not. I'd hate to be riding into Apache country with as cowardly a bully boy as poor old Walter Howard. But getting back to him, and how come I finally had to stand up to him in front of all the girls, it's been my sad experience that sooner or later you have to, no matter how big they may be or how scared you might feel. For as you likely know, the bully boy's brain don't work the way of most mankind. So there's no way anyone natural can reason with or even satisfy the sons-of-bitches. Sweet talk just inspires 'em to act more silly, and giving in to 'em just makes 'em crowd you for even more, until sooner or later you just have to stand up to the rascal. Having tried the other ways to get along with the breed, I decided young it made more sense to just do or die and get it over with.''

Hamp Ferris laughed louder than Seth felt the situation called for, and declared, "You sure talk big for such a pretty little thang, Jersey Lilly. Is it understood that, should we stroll down Lover's Lane to Fist City, it's to be a strictly fist affair, with neither knives nor guns nor other dirty tricks?''

Seth snorted in disgust, and replied, "Grow up. This is Apache country, not a schoolyard, and we're both packing six-guns, real ones, not cap pistols.''

Ferris said uncertainly, "Yeah, but I ain't sure I want to kill you all the way just to show you who's the boss around here.''

Seth shrugged and said, "Don't mess with me unless your intentions are honorable then. The only boss I recognize in these parts is the one who's paying me, and I'd be mighty dumb to fistfight *him*, seeing we're both grown gun-toters.''

Ferris scowled, and said, "Now that's mighty girlish talk, even coming from a milkmaid knowed as the Jersey Lilly. Where I come from real men ain't afraid to fight fair and square with their pure fists.''

Seth smiled thinly, and stated flatly, "It's a good thing we're not where you come from then. I'd likely have my head handed to me in a bruised condition if I went up against a moose your size bare-knuckled. Seeing you have the edge on me in inches, pounds, and reach, I'd best inform you where we stand right here, where neither of us come from.''

The gesture wasn't lost on Ferris when Seth took one step back to fall into the instinctive stance of a gun-fighter, the opposite way a fistfighter positions his feet and upper torso, unless he boxes southpaw with his right hand leading. Ferris gulped, and said, "Hold on now, Jersey Lilly."

But Seth cut in, "You hold on, and get the wax outten your ears. I'm neither scared enough to lick your boots nor dumb enough to volunteer as your private punching bag. So back off or slap leather. For I'm on my way over to yon fire for some coffee now, and to tell the truth I don't much care whether you aim to get the hell outten my way or get it over with for keeps here and now!"

Hamp Ferris grumbled, "Aw, hell, ain't you got no sense of humor at all?" and turned away to get there first, much faster. Seth had to stay put a short spell as he willed his pulse to stop pounding so serious. He lit a cheroot to steady his breathing as well before joining the others around the fire. As the match flared he spied Virgin Joe staring at him sort of chalk-faced from the chest-high brush just north of the wagon trace. Seth almost dropped his match to draw before he recognized the shorter and older Nevada rider in time to go on lighting his smoke.

As he did so Virgin Joe stepped out of the chaparral to join him, saying, "Pinto sent me to find out what was keeping you boys. When I noticed I was heading into a lover's quarrel, I felt it wiser to circle some."

Seth broke the match stem to make certain it was out before he dropped it to the dust, quietly asking how much Virgin Joe might have heard just now.

Virgin Joe shrugged, and replied, "More than I've call to repeat, if that's what you mean."

Seth said, "That's what I mean. I may have cooled his ardor as far as I'm concerned, and you know what they say about letting sleeping dogs lie."

Virgin Joe grimaced, and replied, "They lie even stiller with a couple of bullets in 'em, and you're never going to have a better chance than the one you just gave away, old son."

Seth laughed incredulously, and demanded, "Hold on, you heard him decline my kind offer. What was I supposed to do when he just turned his back on me, blow it full of holes?"

Virgin Joe asked, "Why not? You just warned him not to mess with you with his fists, and we both know he packs a Remington .45 with double action and a filed-off front sight in case he wants to get it out sudden."

They mounted up again in about an hour and rode on through the darkness and chaparral until the false dawn commenced to pearl the skyline behind them to the east. This time it was Elmo Dawson in the flesh who suggested they scout up a place to hole up through the coming daylight hours, observing, "We have to be close enough to the Hatchets for many a hostile to be gazing and grinning this way in anticipation, right?"

But their Indian guide pointed on ahead with his Winchester to inform them, "We can make it to the Butterfield station by the waters of Ntayl before there is enough light to see far. The station will give us plenty shade as well as all the sweetwater we and all these horses need."

"Unless your Apache pals are waiting for us ahint them thick 'dobe walls!" Hamp Ferris objected.

The older Indian turned in his saddle to regard the loudmouth with the enthusiasm of a house-proud spinster of the white-eyed persuasion staring at cobwebs in a corner. He nonetheless politely replied, "If any *friends* of mine were out this summer, I would not be leading you to shade and water. I would be wearing paint across my face, and you would have the *right* to call me and my people Apache. But hear me, Apache means enemy mixed with something like greaser or gringo in the tongue of the Pima, who have never liked us for some reason. We call ourselves Na Déné.''

Then he added with a rather feline twinkle in his wide-set sloe eyes, ''But hear me, if you would rather have me for an enemy than the only one who knows where you are going, just keep it up.''

Elmo Dawson raised his own voice to snap, ''That's enough outten both you boys, damn it! We're wasting time here, arguing like an infernal flock of hens with the sun-ball fixing to come up any minute.''

Benny nodded and heeled his bay forward. As the others fell in behind Dawson growled at Ferris, ''I want you to leave old Benny be. That's an order.''

''I don't trust him far as I can smell him,'' grumbled the unshaven and not-too-tidy Ferris, adding, ''Damned if I have to be nice to him!''

To which Dawson answered flatly, ''Get off my pony and walk back to town then. Benny knows the way to the mine, which is more than any of the rest of you can say. So just study up on which of you I may need most, hear?''

Ferris protested, ''Aw, hell, boss, you know it must be more'n twenty miles back to Deming from here!''

Dawson chuckled dryly, and said, ''It's nice to see you do know that much. Are you sure you was telling me true about your days on the Goodnight-Loving Trail? Cow-boy?''

Ferris grumbled, ''Well, sure I rid that far-flung cattle trail, both ways, more'n once, and I don't recall no *Indians* riding with us. Not on our side, leastways. They say it was Comanche got poor old Oliver Loving that time, and . . ."

But Dawson told the erstwhile Texas drover to spare him the ancient history, and Ferris lapsed into sullen silence. Behind him, Seth Grant was sorely tempted to ask Ferris more about wild Indians along that cattle trail, wherever it had been. He felt sort of left out when these more western gents tossed cryptic remarks about people, places, and events he's never heard about back along the Third River.

But Seth didn't ask. He knew Ferris would think he was trying to butter up to him by offering him such a chance to brag. Natural bullies didn't seem to understand others being nice to them for no reason in particular, which was likely what made 'em natural bullies in the first place.

As the stars above winked out in an ever-lightening sky, Seth saw they were in much more rolling country, covered with higher brush punctuated here and there by mesquite grown big as orchard trees and stalks of that funny stuff he'd been noticing since he was rolling down through Texas aboard the train. Dropping back until he was even with Virgin Joe, he asked quietly, "Do you have a name for that thing over yonder as looks like a giant bristle brush on a shaggy handle thicker than my fool leg?"

Virgin Joe nodded. "They call it Spanish Bayonet or yucca around here. It's some dusty breed of the onion family, and it grows all sorts of odd ways, depending on just where. From about here back to the Brazos it grows sort of lollipop, like so. Further off to the northwest it grows all branchy, like a tree, and so the Mormons calls it Joshua tree. Just to be contrary it grows most places with no bottom stalk at all, from the Mex border up Canada way. It's more use to the Indians than it's ever been to us. They split them stiff green spines for a thread a lot like linen. Some say they make soap outten the roots, whilst others say they can eat 'em. Never having tried yucca neither way, I keeps an open mind on the subject.''

Seth said he would, too, and as they rode on Virgin Joe pointed out the aptly named catsclaw and other, less ferociously spined brush of the semi-arid range. Hardly anything but grass seemed to grow out this way without bearing arms. Virgin Joe said one branch of grass called cheat was a fire hazard, while a succulent, waist-high forb with no thorns at all to guard its juicy green leaves was the notorious loco weed. Virgin Joe gazed about, as if disappointed, as he added, "Jimson weed's even worse, but I don't see no jimson around right now.''

As they topped another rise Seth spied the low sod roofing of the Butterfield station their Indian guide had mentioned. Farther off, but not really that far, the first beams of sunlight were painting the raw peaks of the Hatchets pink. This close it was easy to see how they'd gotten their name. A southward extension of the somewhat higher Rocky Mountains to the north, they did resemble a jumble of giant stone axes with their sharp edges rising every which way to rip the bellies out of unwary clouds. It was still too dark to make out details lower than the higher sunlit rimrocks. The thought of sloe eyes staring down from painted faces inspired someone to call out, "What are we waiting for? Let's git under cover afore them heathen spot us out here like roaches on a kitchen floor!''

But before old Benny could say it, Seth heard someone blurting, "Don't lope your mounts, damn it! Rising dust can be seen miles further than elephants, and this wagon trace is dusty as hell!''

Then he realised who'd yelled that and felt his ears redden as everyone seemed to be staring at him at once. Hamp Ferris snorted, "Well, now, listen to the fine old Indian scout from the frontier state of New Jersey!''

But while more than one of the others laughed, Elmo

Dawson said, "Makes sense. Slow and easy does it. Benny, you want to ride in ahead in case someone you'd be better able to reason with got there first?"

Benny shook his head, and said, "No. If there is anyone there now, they would shoot at me before they'd shoot at you. Hear me, neither Naiche nor Goyalka would be dumb enough to make a stand behind walls in such open country, even if they didn't have more than one cavalry regiment out after them."

Dawson rose in his stirrups for a slightly better view of the layout ahead before he decided, "Makes sense. No stock in the corral out back, and we know the stage line shut down days ago."

Then Dawson decided, "Benny's got a point about dark meat. How do you feel about scouting ahead for us, Grant?"

Seth was more startled than scared by the order. He knew it was an order, unless he wanted to look like a Jersey Lilly indeed. So he just hauled the Winchester he'd been issued from its saddle boot, levered a round into its chamber, and spurred his buckskin barb forward, neither raising dust nor reining in sneaksome. The long, low, and somehow brooding stage station couldn't have been a quarter-mile to ride. It felt more like a day's journey, with no cover, but all things good and bad must end, and so later he dismounted near the front veranda, loosely looped the reins around a handy hitching post, and kicked open a door to chase the muzzle of his Winchester inside.

As he saw something moving in a far corner of the dark interior he fired and had a rat blown half in two as he snapped the breech open and shut on another round. So even though that had been the only dependent of the Butterfield Stage Line still on the premises, as far as Seth could see, he saw all the others had taken cover when he finally stepped out into the open to wave them on in with his long-gun.

They took their time making up their minds. Once they saw nobody was forcing him to act as a decoy, they made up for it by moving in faster than Seth had. But as he watched them moving against the sunrise neither the eight other riders nor the four pack mules led by Little Dipper kicked up dust much higher than the top twigs of the chaparral all around. As Elmo Dawson—in the lead—reined in he asked Seth what they had here. Seth shrugged, and said, "Eight rooms of empty shell. The Butterfield boys really overloaded their wagons when they blue-streaked into the county seat."

So Dawson allowed their own stock would be cooler as well as out of sight in the passengers' dining room. Seth pitched in to help Little Dipper and Virgin Joe water and crack-corn the riding and pack stock. It was his notion to unsaddle them and rub them down as well. When Little Dipper pointed out they'd just have to cinch up all those fool riding and pack saddles again at sunset, Seth snorted in disgust, and asked, "No fooling, Little Dipper, did you really work as a cowhand in your misspent youth, or were you one of those gents who peddles pony rides to city kids when school's out for the summer?"

Virgin Joe laughed, and explained, "He means that's one hell of a way to treat a mount, Little Dipper. A horse ain't a bicycle you can just lean agin' a fence betwixt the times you ride it, you know."

Little Dipper still grumbled as he helped them unsaddle and rub down the twelve brutes. But at least he helped, and when they'd finished he grimaced, and asked, "Satisfied?"

To which Seth replied, "Not hardly. But since it was Elmo, not you, as put this remuda together, I'd best talk to him about it."

Suiting actions to his words, he toted his stock saddle into the stripped-down main salon to find Hamp Ferris, Kid Wagner, and Big Dipper hunkered around the beehive fireplace in one corner. When he asked where the boss might be, Big Dipper said to try the pump shed out back. Hamp Ferris asked Seth if he had shot the rat they'd just kicked out the front door. When Seth allowed he had, Ferris laughed too loudly, and demanded, "How come, Jersey Lilly? Did it raise its fists to you?"

The others seemed to find that amusing, too. Seth said, "If you boys mean to start a fire there, for whatever dumb reason, you'd best check with Dawson and old Benny first."

"You just ask their permit to fly a kite," snapped Ferris, adding, "We're using cheat grass for tinder and dead mesquite branches for fuel, and if you knew squat about either you'd know neither puts enough smoke in the air to spy from any distance."

Big Dipper soothed, "The 'dobe walls in here have took a damp chill from the past few nights, and we got us some taters to bake besides."

Seth shrugged, said he still thought it dumb to build any kind of fire in the face of the heat they'd be having by noon, and headed on back with his saddle and possibles. He dropped them off in a small room that had likely been a pantry when this place had still been in business and ambled on back through the gutted kitchen. Just outside the back door he spied the smaller shed of sun-silvered wood, and the cussing and banging coming from it could only mean he'd found the pump shed Big Dipper had mentioned. Inside he found Elmo Dawson cranking, cussing, and kicking at the cast-iron pump in the center of the dirt floor as, behind him, old Benny squatted in a far corner, half asleep.

Seth said, "That stock you begged, bought, or stole

from somewhere is in piss-poor shape for one night's ride out of town, Elmo. The saddle pads and blankets haven't been cleaned for a coon's age, and you keep rubbing wool that filthy into hide that's worn and sweaty, you're fixing to have some might sick critters, sudden.''

Dawson said, ''That's the least of our problems right now. I hired enough water bags to last us a couple of days betwixt springs and old Benny yonder tells me we'll just make the next water if we leave here with our bellies as well as all our bags and canteens chock full!''

''Can't you get that pump to work?'' asked Seth innocently.

From Dawson's reaction one might have thought he'd asked what kind of a lay his dear old mother had been. Dawson took off his hat, threw it down in the dirt, and kicked it out the open doorway. He roared, ''Would I be all sweated up like this if the infernal pump wasn't dry as a spider's belly button? It'd be even drier if I hadn't wasted half a canteen trying to prime the damned thing, and now the damned water we've left just ain't going to last us long enough!''

Seth reached in his pocket as he asked Dawson to stand aside and let him have a look-see. The burlier Dawson did so, but growled, ''What do you suspect you can do about it? Are you a mechanic as well as a milkmaid, Grant?''

Seth unfolded the screwdriver blade of his pocketknife as he replied, ''Not hardly, but you do learn to sort of haywire all sorts of notions back together, living on eighty acres growing this and that. I doubt the Butterfield crew could have removed the innards and left this fine detachable handle. So it's likely a dried out valve leather, as you suspected, or, even more likely, a pebble sucked up the tube by enthusiasticated pumping.''

Elmo Dawson watched with interest, and old Benny even opened one eye, as Seth got to work with his screwdriver. It wasn't easy to start the rusted-in and painted-over retaining screw, and even after he'd managed that, he'd have never gotten the pump head off if he hadn't been strong as well as skilled in the arcane arts of country tinkering. But once he was able to get at the simple leather flap valve Elmo had already softened for him, he found that sure enough a bit of bedrock and a gob of mud had been holding the flap open both ways and preventing the vacuum required to suck groundwater up the tube. A couple of scrapes with his knife blade dealt with that and the pump head went back together a heap easier than it had come apart. Old Benny actually got back up to watch in admiration as Seth worked the pump to send water gushing out the side of the shed into the watering trough that led over to the now-empty corral. Elmo Dawson slapped Seth on the back, and said, "By gum, you surely are a handy young cuss. What was that you said about saddle blankets afore?"

Seth repeated his charges. The older westerner shrugged and told him, "Matter of fact, neither me nor your average top hand off a cow spread has to know all that much about such petty details. It's up to the wrangler, who's usually a Mex or nigger in these parts, to see that each top hand's pony is saddled proper and ready to ride come morning. Your average vaquero rides a fresh and different pony ever' morning during busy times on the spread. So he'd never have time for much riding if he had to tend that many ponies his personal self."

Seth shrugged, and said, "Be that as it may, and seeing we have plenty of water here and now, what say I give all the pads and blankets a good washing out before we ride on this evening? They'll dry out fluffsome in plenty of time, hung over them corral poles under the sun all afternoon."

"I doubt we got that much soap betwixt the nine of

us," said Dawson. Then he shrugged, and added, "Might help to get some of the sweat out, leastways, if you don't mind sweating that hard your ownself. Are you supposed to be some sort of horse doctor as well as a farm mechanic and the gunslick I thought I was hiring to begin with?"

Seth allowed that you just couldn't know enough, farming eighty acres with neither a Mex nor a nigger on hand to do your chores for you. So Dawson laughed, slapped him on the back again, and told him he was free to wash everyone's socks as well, if that was his pleasure.

As the other white man and the old Indian turned away, Seth stopped Benny. Seth said, "One of the other boys told me you can get soap out of those big yucca plants. You'd be the one who's word I'd take on that."

The tawny Chiricahua shook his head, and said, "Not the big ones. The ones that grow right out of the ground, like grass. The spines all look the same, just as Na Déné all look the same to you people, but neither we nor the yuccas are exactly the same. Fill the trough while I go into the chaparral to gather the right kind of yucca. You have some good thoughts, but by my gods and your Jesus-mother you have a lot to learn!"

Seth felt no call to argue that point, albeit he found it mighty annoying when Hamp Ferris and a couple of the others followed him back out with all the saddle pads and blankets to offer such useful suggestions as posting a sign reading "NO TICKEE NO WASHEE!"

They got tired of watching him soak dirty wool before Benny got back with a double armful of roots that tried to look like big onions and carrots at the same time. Dumping them nearby the old Indian said, "Too much water. Hear me, spread blankets wet on ground. Rub in wood ashes. Rub yucca roots all over until you get foam like soap suds. Do this until yucca all used up. Soak blankets in water a while. Drain troughs. Fill troughs. Do this until water is clear. Do this by yourself. The women of my people do such work. The men of my people don't. I have spoken.''

Seth figured the Chiricahua meant it when he suddenly found himself alone out back, doing the considerable chore he'd volunteered for with his big mouth. Virgin Joe came out half an hour later with some beans and coffee for him. He let everything soak while he wolfed down the Spartan breakfast. Then he rinsed out the tin cup and plate while he was at it, set them aside to sun-dry, and got back to work. It was pushing noon and it felt like it by the time Seth had all their saddle pads and blankets draped over corral poles to dry. He limped back inside to see what they were serving for noon dinner. But everyone seemed to be fast asleep, save for old Benny, who was missing entire. So once he'd determined their Indian guide was standing guard on the roof above them Seth unfurled his bedroll, lay atop it with his duds on and his gunbelt and head pillowed on the saddle, and shut his eyes to see if he could catch a few winks.

He figured he must have slept, even though it didn't feel like it. Elmo Dawson kicked open the door to yell, ''Get up and eat your damned grub, kid. The sun's going down, and we're fixing to go on!''

Seth started to protest; that hardly seemed possible. Then he saw how hellfire-red the light outside his bitty room had turned and sat up. He winced in pain as he saw he'd moved a mite fast for a lad who'd gone to sleep sweaty on a hard floor. But what the hell, he was sure to feel even worse after another night in the saddle. So why sob like a sissy this early?

The next morning found them far off the usual routes through the Hatchets, well into Apacheria proper. As they made day camp in the demi-Eden their Indian guide had led them to, Seth found his surroundings surprising in more ways than one. The mountain glen was sweet smelling and well shaded against the coming glare of the June sun by timber grown tall as the elms shading many a pleasant street back east. But the earth and fallen leaves around their roots were bone dry, and when Seth asked Benny where the nearest mountain rill might be, the Indian told him, "Two days ride. Maybe more. Many springs dry up in summer on this slope of these hills. Did you think I would be dumb enough to lead you to a well-watered camp site with both Naiche and Goyalka out, not far from here?"

Seth said he followed the old Chiricahua's drift, and in truth it was still a nice campsite, provided one had brought plenty of water along. Pinto's coffee was a mite bitter, and his beans were getting monotonous. But the one thing to be said for plain camp fare was that you didn't have to pack as much along when it wasn't all that delicious. So Seth got down just enough to satisfy his gut rumbles and sat on a sandstone slab to smoke, staring thoughtfully up at the even thicker blue haze rising from Pinto's modest fire. By now Seth understood why men traveling through Apacheria preferred to light fires in broad daylight. It made more sense as soon as one considered that, while thick smoke could be seen from far off, thin smoke might be missed, and the human eye could, and likely would, fix on a match struck three miles away after dark. Watching the thin woodsmoke curling through cottonwood leaves fluttering forty or more feet above them Seth felt almost sure it dissipated well below the treetops. But feeling almost sure might not be sure enough in Apache country, so, seeing he had nothing better to do in any case, Seth picked up his Winchester, rose to his feet, and started up the dry canyon to make sure. Nobody asked where he was going. Even cow hands considered it rude to heed the call of nature within sight of the grub on the fire.

A few moments later Seth had the narrow canyon all to himself; fluttering leaves were all around. The country was new to him, but being a country boy, he wasn't as spooked as some might have been by the way the cottonwoods whispered to him even though there wasn't a breath of breeze at ground level. The lizards and such as skittered off through the dry leaves every now and again took more getting used to. But you hardly ever saw what was skittering ahead of you back in the Wachungs of New Jersey, and a snakebite out here couldn't hurt you much worse than a snakebite back there. Uncle Bob had told him, on a visit home when everyone had been a heap younger, that no matter where one went in this great land there were really only four kinds of snakes you had to worry about. Once you learned to recognize a rattlesnake, a copperhead, a cottonmouth, and a coral, you didn't have to give a fig what any other kind of snake you saw might be. As to lizards, Uncle Bob had said there was only one kind out here or anywhere else other than the Gila or Mex beaded. Those you really had to run from. So when Seth flushed a squat ugly horned toad he just let it run from him, even though he'd never seen such an odd-looking lizard in his life, up to now.

It soon became obvious this twisty, tree-lined canyon ran way up into the mountains. So, skinning the cat another way, Seth started up one wall. It wasn't easy. It wouldn't have been easy had he left his Winchester down below with the lizards. But seeing the walls were neither sheer nor devoid of hand- and toe-holds, he was able to work himself up about as far as the cottonwoods grew. From there, looking down the way he'd come, he saw no smoke from Pinto's fire. So he grunted in satisfaction and began to work his way down. Then the morning sun flashed on something for just one firefly wink, and that was enough, once Seth's eye had been drawn to something darker than shade should be, sitting or squatting in a clump of hillside mesquite, mayhaps another quarter-mile west.

Seth took a good bearing on the mysterious flasher's position and quietly moved down below the treetops. Once back on the sandy bottom of the canyon it was an easy chore to ease on up, say, a hundred yards beyond the cleft the mesquite clump was growing out of, and simply work his own way behind the sneaky cuss with his Winchester. He knew it had to be another human being. Sunlight didn't flash so on anything but glass or metal, and not even Ned Buntline's wild west magazines suggested wilder critters sporting eyeglasses or silver buckles. He worked his way higher, behind the mesquite, and when he found a natural ledge leading downward toward it, he levered a round into the chamber and eased on in, the muzzle of his long-gun trained on the bush, ready for just about anything.

But what happened next was the sound of a single action six-gun being cocked behind him as someone said, in English, "Just keep going to where there's room to turn around, son. We'll both find it more comfortable discussing your future in the shade of them old mesquites where I left my possibles as well."

Seth gulped, and said, without looking back, "You sure slickered me, mister. How did you know I'd spotted you, hid out so swell like that?"

The man chuckled dryly, and replied, "You get so's you can tell. You're not bad yourself, boy. I thought I was hid pretty good, so high and shadesome."

Seth confessed, "I'd have never spotted you if the rising sun hadn't winked on something shiny you have on." So the man with the drop on him sighed, and said, sheepishly, "That's one on me then. I'm sure glad it was you and not a damned Na Déné as spotted me. I've always found them boys harder to get the drop on, once they do. Who might you be, by the way, and what are you and them other white eyes doing up here in these hills with Naiche and Goyalka at it again?''

As they worked their way along the ledge Seth explained who he was and what he and the others thought they were doing up in these hills at a time like this. By the time he'd finished they'd made it to the sort of eagle's nest his captor had fashioned among the twisted stems of the mesquite clump. Seth heard him uncock and reholster his six-gun as he decided, ''We'd best not kill one another after all, seing the Na Déné would just laugh like hell at any winner. I'd be Tom Horn, scouting for Miles on my lonesome now that old Al Sieber's been crippled with a bullet in his dainty left hoof. I was wondering which band would be camped this far from water when I spied your smoke against the sunrise. I'm sure glad you came up to tell me about it. Might have wasted me a whole day scouting other white eyes, ain't that a bitch?''

Seth allowed it sure was as he got to turn around for his first look at the army scout. Tom Horn was a lean but nice-looking gent in his middle to late twenties. His eyes stared at everything in sight more like those of a good mouser than a wise old owl. His mustache didn't make him look as ferocious as it was doubtless supposed to. Seth got the impression Horn could be an easygoing pal or a deadly enemy without expending much heavy thought on which it was to be.

Seth took out the fancy cigar Elmo Dawson had bestowed upon him, saying, ''I've been saving this claro for an occasion.'' But Horn shook his head and went on chewing what Seth had assumed to be tobacco before Horn said, ''I don't smoke. I chaws bacon when I can get it. Steadies the hands just as fine as chewing tobacco, and you don't have to worry about where you spit because it don't make you sick when you swallers bacon juice. You want some?''

Seth said he'd just as soon try out Dawson's claro, adding that he hoped it was safe to do so up here, of course. Horn nodded soberly, and replied, ''It must be. If there was any Chiricahua within miles, they'd have hit you boys by now.''

Seth repressed a shudder as they both sat down, and he got the cigar going at last. As they filled one another in it developed Horn didn't know old Benny, or Bay-nay as the Na Déné-speaking Horn agreed the man's name was pronounced. He'd heard of Chief Loco, of course, and allowed it was evidence the old cuss wasn't really crazy that he'd refused to come out again this summer. Horn said, ''When even the other war leaders refuse to come out, that's as good as saying the war is over. Only the padres messed up Goyalka's poor head when they baptized him after Saint Jerome, or Geronimo as they say it in Spanish. Old Goyolka can't make up his mind whether he's a wild Indian or a Mex bandit. So he behaves a mite like both and that's what makes it hard for the army to figure what he'll try next.''

''What about the other chief, Naiche?'' Seth asked.

Horn said, ''Oh, he's just a mean little kid. Wants the gals to look up to him like they did his dad, Cochise, and his even meaner grandad, Mangas Colorados. Naiche's not as clever as Goyalka by half, but he's even meaner, and nobody's ever accused Goyalka of being softhearted. You don't want either band to capture you alive, boy. Make sure you've always got one last bullet saved for yourself, and, when the time comes, don't hesitate to put the muzzle in your mouth like a candy cane and pull the trigger, pronto. They considers it real brag to take a prisoner alive, and they can move in on you like spit across the top of a hot stove, see?''

Seth repressed a shudder and said he'd already made up his mind not to be taken alive. Then he said, "They might find it tougher to take *any* of us alive, seeing we have one of their own guiding us."

Horn shrugged, and said, "Mebbe so. Like I said, I don't know a thing about your Bay-nay. You say he was with Loco when they run over that Mex gold camp?"

Seth nodded soberly, but said, "He says his own band's not on the warpath this summer, and I see no reason to doubt him. But seeing him and the other boys might be worried about my taking so long out here I'd best get on back. Would you like to come along for, say, some coffee, Mr. Horn?"

The army scout shook his head, and said, "I'd best get on back to General Miles afore he sends someone out looking for *me*. With Al Sieber stove up I'm his one and only senior scout, see?"

Seth nodded, and said, "You told me about your boss scout getting wounded. How did it happen? In a skirmish with those birds you've been chasing?"

Horn shook his head, and answered soberly. "Nope. Al got shot when one of our own Apache scouts turned on him. They do that now and again, you see. It's tough for any of us to say just why."

On their fourth hot day in the Hatchets they got to hole up by a cool, spring-fed stream purling down a lush green glen. This was the first chance they'd had to refill their canteens and water bags since leaving that Butterfield pump, and it made Seth feel more than a little crawly. For by now he'd seen enough of the land to sense how Apacheria worked.

The people known to everyone but themselves as Apache were neither the desert dwellers nor the irregular cavalry some pictured. Raiding most anywhere they could get to for fun and profit, they were still hill folk at heart, and the key to survival in their rumpled patchwork quilt of wooded slopes, raw rimrock, and brush-choked canyons was the simple substance known as water. There just wasn't that much of it in the deceptively green canyon maze this far into high summer, and Seth felt sure the Indians had a pretty good idea where all of it was.

He asked Benny about that after breakfast. They sat side by side on a log, watching the water sparkle as the sun rose higher. The old Indian told him, "The army has this sweetwater on their survey maps. You told us the other day you had met one of their scouts. I think we would have heard some noise by this time if either Naiche or Goyalka was around here. General Miles has mountain artillery with his column. He says he thinks it is dumb to send a rider where a cannon shell can go in Indian country. I think he is right. I know he means it. Maybe that is why neither Loco nor Mangas wanted to come out this time."

The old warrior repressed a sigh and added softly, "Fighting the army is no fun anymore. Since the good fight your people call the Battle of Apache Pass the blue sleeves have learned many things, many, about ambush. Now, when they see a good place for our boys to maybe get set up for them, they shell it from well out of rifle range whether there is anybody there or not."

Seth shifted his weight uncomfortably and pegged a bit of agate into the stream, saying, "Tom Horn sounded like he's still worried about your wilder kinsmen, out there somewheres."

Benny smiled thinly, and replied, "Hear me, if the army really had anything to worry about, I would be out there with them. I am not helping you and Elmo Dawson get rich because you have tamed me like a horse you've roped.

I need to get rich, too, because the old ways don't work any more.''

He smote his own bare thigh with a bony fist and almost snarled, "Hear me. I wished to keep fighting when Loco surrendered to your General Crook four years ago. But how can one man fight alone? Hear me, how can even Naiche and Goyalka hope to go on fighting with at least two cavalry columns out after them and more women and children than warriors in their bands?''

A cutthroat trout broke the surface out on the sun-dappled water. Seth said, "Damn, I sure wish I had me a rod and reel right now, don't you?''

The Indian said, "No. My people don't eat those slimy things like you and less proud red men do. I don't want to live at the San Carlos Agency either. The damned B.I.A. must think we're damned Pueblos. We don't like it up that way.''

Seth tried not to laugh as he replied soberly, "So I've noticed. Seems every time the army gets you birds back on the San Carlos reserve you fly the coop. Some of you, leastways. Do you mind my asking a personal question, Benny?''

The Indian answered simply, "Go ahead. If I don't want to answer, I won't.''

Seth said that sounded fair and continued, "I ain't sure I follow this business about reservations. How come Geronimo rates all those soldiers chasing him every time he leaves whilst you seem free to come and go as you please, no offense?''

Benny looked disgusted, and replied, "I just told you I'm in this for money, too. Neither the B.I.A. nor the army cares if one of us leaves the agency, as long as we obey all your damned laws, as if we were Mexicans or women. Didn't you just hear me say the old ways don't work any more? Naiche and Goyalka are not being hunted because they are Na Déné. They are being hunted because they keep trying to *live* like Na Déné, see?''

Seth brightened, and said, ''I'm commencing to. Your old way of life involved a certain amount of, well, Robin Hood notions allowing for good clean rape and pillage, right?''

Benny nodded innocently, and declared, ''Hear me. In the beginning Raven made my people to prey on Pueblos and other lesser creatures as puma, real wolf, even coyote have the right to. Some say that far to the north, where the days and nights act crazy, there are other people who speak Déné. But in this part of the world only we and the bands you call Navaho for some reason talk as Raven taught us. Nobody else speaks anything like us, nobody. Nobody else understands our customs, or our right to horses, women, and other good things from those who don't know how to talk and fight like real men. So everyone's hand, red or white, is raised against us when we just act like ourselves.''

''I figured the army had a reason for singling out one nation in these parts for its undivided attention,'' Seth said dryly.

Benny nodded and replied, ''I just said the old ways didn't work the way they used to. Those of us who don't wish to live like agency pets or damned farmers have to get money, lots of money, any way the white-eyed law allows. That way a man can wear fine clothes and own pretty horses and women without having to do anything he doesn't want to. Off the reservation he can even drink all the tiswin he wants. You call it whiskey and the Mexicans call it tequila, but we make it even better when we can get the damned Indian agents to leave us alone.''

That trout, or another one, broke the surface again. Benny nodded at it, and said, ''When we all get rich you'll be able to eat all the slimy fish you want and I'll eat pony until my wives and me get fat and beautiful. Nobody in my family has ever died fat, although I had a fat Mexican wife one time. She was a lot of fun. I still miss her. She was killed in a skirmish with the Mescalero many summers ago.''

Seth frowned thoughtfully, and said, ''Correct me if I'm wrong, but ain't the Mescalero another breed of, ah, Na Déné?''

Benny nodded cheerfully, considering, and replied, ''Yes. They have ridden with our Chiricahua against Mexicans from time to time, but mostly we raid one another for horses and guns when either is in short supply. Naturally you never find other Na Déné with inferior stock or weaponry, see?''

Seth grimaced, and said, ''I'm commencing to. Don't your fellow tribesmen have any shame at all when it comes to raiding most anyone you can get the drop on?''

Benny shook his head, and replied, ''Shame is a funny word to use for a man who beats another out of something. Raven made us to feel *proud* at such times. But hear me, don't think we are bad people who have no sense of right and wrong. No Na Déné, even a Mescalero, would steal the pony of another man he knew by name, unless the man was a Mexican that is, and unlike your own kind, none of us, none, would ever trifle with the wife of a comrade in arms.''

''What about the gals you boys just ride off with on occasion?'' asked the bemused white youth.

Benny replied calmly, ''A woman taken from an enemy is a prize of war. Even my Mexican wife understood that, once she'd been beaten, just a little. But once a woman has been claimed by a real man, even if she was a white eyes before he took her, no Na Déné would dream of dishonoring her. We leave that sort of disgusting behavior to you and the Mexicans. Why do you both seem to feel it proves a man is brave if he trifles with another man's wife behind his back? Wouldn't it be braver to just tell the other man he wanted her and then take her?''

Seth laughed and decided, ''I'll go along with you on that, at least. But I can see I have a heap to learn about your people and, seeing you say we're still a good ways from that old camp, what say you teach me some Apache, I mean Na Déné, Benny?''

The older man stared uncertainly at him, then replied in a puzzled tone, ''Why? I speak English, and any Na Déné you meet who don't will be shooting at you, not talking to to you.''

''Even if I'm with you?'' asked the white youth with a worried frown.

To which the old Indian answered blandly, ''Even if you are with me, Loco, Mangas, or any other such person who's made peace with the white eyes. Neither Naiche nor Goyalka would be out this summer against such odds unless they were very cross with *everybody*, *all* of us.''

But over the next few days and nights Seth got the gruff old guide to give him a few lessons in a very difficult lingo indeed. Seth wasn't all that sure he was learning anything, but at least it helped pass the time and gave him some few inklings as to what all the fuss might be about.

The few ''Indian'' words Seth and most whites thought they knew derived, of course, from the Algonquin dialects of the eastern woodland culture, along with a smattering of Iroquoian somewhat mangled in Longfellow's poetic but historically absurd ''Hiawatha.'' So the first thing he learned about Na Déné was that it was totally unrelated to any other language understood by anyone, red or white, in the southwest. After that it got more complicated. Thanks to some Hudson Valley Dutch on his maternal side and some papist Scotch paternal kin who still cussed in the Gaelic, Seth started with the advantage of knowing there was more to learning another lingo than just the sound of new words. Each lingo had its own grammar, or the way the words were strung together, and Na Déné grammar was a pain in the ass.

He'd thought the Gaelic was complicated enough with its verbs always coming first. In Na Déné there seemed to be no such thing as one word for one thing. When asked what the Na Déné would say for a damned horse Benny responded, "What kind of horse, doing what, and is it in sight right now, or are we talking about a horse I stole last summer?"

It seemed you didn't get to say "hello" to anyone either. Benny said he'd had a time getting used to that notion, learning English. For when two of his folk met they either knew one another or they didn't. So what in thunder was the point of saying anything to a man you were fixing to kill, and why did you have to inform a friend you were standing there unless he was blind, in which case it made more sense to tell him who you were and ask him if he needed any help in getting to where he was going.

But if the language lessons failed to teach Seth the Na Déné language, it did serve to give him some sense of the way Benny's people thought. Or at least it warned him they didn't think at all the way one might expect them to. The good-natured old saw about all folk being much the same down deep simply served to cause a heap of misunderstanding between Seth's kind and the American Indian, and even Mexicans, by assuming all too quickly that everyone involved in an argument knew what the argument was really about. Without really understanding Benny and his people, Seth at least had sense enough to know he never would, and that he best be ready for surprises while trying not to offer any with a hasty word or gesture.

The older Indian had, of course, learned way more about the sometimes amusing and often annoying customs of the white eyes, long before he'd met anyone as willing to try to learn his people's ways as Seth. So he got along well enough with most of the others by simply ignoring them as much as possible. They in turn got along with him by sort of pretending he wasn't there, save for Elmo Dawson, who asked the guide lots of questions, and Hamp Ferris, who seemed to find anything an Indian said annoying as hell. Seth was tempted more than once to tell Ferris not to rawhide old Benny. But he knew some of the others might resent it as well if he started giving orders to men he neither fed nor paid. In any case, Elmo Dawson told Ferris to leave the Indian alone more than once, and if Ferris wouldn't listen to their boss who *was* he liable to listen to?

In the end it was Benny himself Ferris listened to or should have sooner. It happened just at sunrise their sixth day out from that Butterfield station when their guide called a halt and hole-up in a dry and dusty boulder-strewn canyon. As they dismounted to water the ponies with the little tepid water left in the rubberized canvas bags, Ferris protested. "I ain't about to spend a whole day baking in this sandstone oven! Just feel how hot it is in here already, with the sun barely riz! Come high noon with the sun ball glaring straight down at us, we'll be lucky if we ain't all dead of heat stroke along with our livestock!"

Seth just hated to agree with the loudmouthed Ferris about anything, even when he seemed to be right. So it was Elmo Dawson who came over, leading his bay for lack of anything to tie the reins to as he cautiously asked, "Is this the best you can do us, chief?"

Benny nodded curtly, and said, "We are close to that gold camp, close. Tomorrow, maybe the next day, you will see the blue streak I told you about. It will lead us right to the yellow iron those Mexicans were digging when we jumped them four summers ago. I was not the only one who rode with Loco that time. If anyone who rode with us now rides with Naiche or Goyalka, he will know about that blue streak along one canyon wall and what it leads to. Hear me, this would not be a good time to make camp within a night's ride of that easy sign to remember. My Na Déné brothers may not care about the yellow iron, but don't bet on a Christian convert, like the one the padres named Geronimo, not having any use for dinero.''

"Didn't you and Loco get any gold they'd already dug?" asked Dawson with a thin smile.

Benny said, "Of course. I told you my people didn't *mine* ore. I never said they were stupid. You can buy many bullets, many, for a pinch of yellow iron. But be quiet and let me finish. Even if my Na Déné brothers don't want the mine, they'll have plenty use, plenty, for the valley it lies in. I told you it was not on any map. The Mexicans who found the place in the days Mexico claimed these hills saw no need to pay the Royal Fifth the Mexicans still claimed after they said they didn't want their king in Spain anymore. So I don't think the army knows about that valley and, hear me, there is plenty of water, grass, and firewood, even game, in the side canyons all around. I think if I were Naiche or Goyalka, I would wish to hold that valley for the rest of this summer at least. This side of the Hatchets will get hotter and drier before they get cooler and wetter. By the time you call July only a few springs, few, will still be flowing. Not even Naiche can hold out up here with no water. But the water near that Mexican mine flows on into the time you call October, and by then the clouds will hang heavy among the rimrocks and the dry times will be over until this time next year.''

The old highlander swung his Winchester barrel expansively at the barren cliffs all around them to add, ''We should stay here until we can move on again, because Ferris with the big mouth is right about this being a terrible place to camp. If it was any better we might have others joining us here, not for breakfast. Even though both Naiche and Goyalka lead small bands, there are only nine of us, nine.''

Elmo Dawson grimaced, and said, ''All right. But I'm holding you to your mysterious blue streak turning up damned sudden. How did it get there anyways? Might them Mexicans have painted it along a canyon wall to show the way?''

Benny snorted, and said, ''That would have been dumb, even for a Mexican. We only saw the blue streak on this side after we'd hit them from the other. Nobody painted it. It's just there, running for maybe ten of your miles along one canyon wall.''

Dawson nodded sagely, and said, ''Sounds like slate layered betwixt lighter sandstone. Pinto? You want to scout up something to make a fire with, mayhaps a pack-rat nest betwixt some of them boulders?''

Pinto swore, told Virgin Joe to give him a hand, and headed up the canyon, muttering to himself. Ferris stepped closer to Benny, his mount's reins in hand, to demand, ''Do something with my pony, Apache, seeing you're so smart about camping in these damned old hills of your'n!''

The older man stared disdainfully at the bigger white rider, and soberly replied, ''I have told you to leave me alone. I have told you more than once. I am not going to tell you again. I mean that. I have spoken.''

Ferris laughed mockingly and moved a step closer, asking, ''What if I don't want to leave you alone, Apache? What if I just whup your red ass and teach you not to sass your betters, hear?''

Benny must have heard. He whipped the muzzle of his

Winchester up until it was almost scraping Hamp's belt buckle and pulled the trigger.

As Hamp Ferris jackknifed in the middle around the expanding cotton blossom of black-powder smoke, his shirt set afire by the point-blank muzzle blast, Seth heard himself yelling "No!" even as everyone but him seemed to be aiming at once. Then anything anyone had to say was drowned out in the rattle of small-arms fire that crackled and echoed up and down the dry stone walls of the canyon until there was so much smoke nobody could see what in thunder he might be shooting at.

As the sulfurous haze thinned to the same shade of blue as watered milk somebody whistled, and somebody else said, "You can say that again!" For while Hamp Ferris just smouldered and twitched on the sunbaked gravel, old Benny had been shot to a mighty limp and lifeless mess of shredded beef with plenty of catsup spread all over it. Kid Wagner, first to start reloading his six-gun from his belt loops, muttered, "That'll larn him to gun a white man!"

Seth started to say something and decided he'd best not. As his eyes met those of Elmo Dawson, the gold seeker who'd hired both the dead men sighed, and said, "Well, I tried to tell old Hamp, and I reckon we just had to do what was right by him in the end."

Seth swallowed the green taste in his mouth, and muttered, "Whether it was right or not, nobody can say it was all that smart. How do you figure on finding that gold mine after blowing the poor old cuss to hash, boss?"

Elmo Dawson looked stricken but quickly recovered, and said, "Hell, you just heard Benny telling me there was a sort of big blue streak blazing the trail ten miles afore you get to the infernal place! All we have to do is find such a streak somewhere's out ahead and just follow it up or down the canyon, knowing the mine has to be at one end or the other."

He glanced down again at the two cadavers, shrugged, and decided, "We'd best move up or down afore the heat stinks these old boys up on us. Looking on the brighter side, Hamp was a pest, and that's two less shares to divvy up once we find the gold."

Everyone but Seth seemed cheered by this. It was Seth who pointed out, "We've got fewer guns and no translator if we run into anyone else who likes noise. You call that the brighter side?"

They sweated out the long hot day in the canyon, made their way south along the natural grain of the hills through the cool night that followed, then Elmo Dawson announced it was time to do things a mite different.

With their Apache guide gone they'd have to seek his mysterious blue streak by daylight. Since the late Benny had hardly been the only Apache in Apacheria, they moved quiet as church mice with lookouts not only posted on the crags above but sort of leapfrogging ahead as the main party moved the stock and supplies through the bewilderment below.

It was after he'd scrambled up a hogback that Seth began to gain an even better sense of this particular stretch of the continental divide. The monstrous slabs of rock that had likely inspired earlier travelers to dub these hills the Hatchet Range rose gently from the east to climax in scary cliffs of jagged rimrock facing the ever-higher waves of shale and sandstone to the west. Seth hardly needed a contour map to surmise that on the far side of the central granite spine the slabs would slope the opposite way.

Whatever had pushed the continental divide up had done so at a mighty slow pace by human reckoning. Water courses already running across the grain of the budding ranges had just kept running, eroding their beds ever deeper or maybe just keeping them where they'd been to begin with. It was as if the land had risen slowly against a stationary but stubborn band saw, so that now canyons great and small ran smack through long, steep ridges at right angles, acute angles, and just about any angle one might shake a stick at. While Seth still sensed that a born and bred native of this busted-up country would have a better feel for the rugged hills, he kept an eye peeled for movement on any of the other high points all around. He gained a certain comfort from the fact that now he might just be able to find his way *out* of this mess on his own if he ever had to. A water course running down-slope through the face of a sheer cliff was likely aimed more or less east. Seth felt no call to work his way any further west than the situation really called for.

But their search took them ever higher into the hills as they scouted in vain for anything answering to old Benny's description of a guideline ten miles long.

The jumbled boulders and bedrock of the Hatchets came in many colors, from granite gray through various shades of tan and ocher to brick red. Here and there a layer of shale that looked *sort* of blue, or at least blue-gray in contrast to the warmer autumn shades of stone, ran as much as say a quarter-mile at the same angle as all the other tilted layers only to end when that particular slab's western rim busted off in the middle of nowhere. It was Seth, riding with Elmo Dawson for a spell as Kid Wagner took his turn as a mountain goat, who noted that the latest layer of shale they'd found couldn't be what the old Indian had been talking about. When Dawson demanded in a sullen tone where Seth had studied geology, the younger easterner calmly answered, ''Don't have to be a rock hound if you listen with both ears. Benny said him and those other Indians spied that streak he mentioned running along *one wall* of the canyon they were riding *down*, meaning roughly west to east. Anyone can see this particular layer of more lavender than blue-gray shale crops out on *both* walls of this canyon.''

Dawson snorted in annoyance, and replied, "Well, of course it does. Can't you see how this canyon was cut through one big layer cake of shale and sandstone, boy?''

Seth said stubbornly, "Benny never said his blue streak ran along both walls. He said one. He didn't say much unless what he was saying meant something serious. That layer of long-dried-out clay wouldn't strike anyone who knew this country well as serious, Elmo. Shale crops out all through this country, common as the almost useless crap it is. Even if it was an unusual shade, which it ain't, it can't run anything like ten miles at that angle before it runs into a heap of sky. I vote we keep looking for what Benny described to you, a stripe running *level*, and to hell with the tilted rock layers, on one wall, not both, and a bright enough blue to attract the notion of a passing rider with more important things, like the U.S. Cavalry, on his mind.''

Dawson sighed, smiled despite himself, and decided, "We'll swing south some more once we bust through the high side of this hogback. I was listening to the old heathen hard as you. But I still can't picture what he could have been talking about. There's no sensible way nature could have painted a long blue steak on only one side of a canyon wall against the natural grain of the rock layers, and I'll be damned if I can see a *human* hand that industrious.''

He clucked his mount into a faster walk, adding, "Say some long-gone greaser wanted to blaze him a trail to that mine, he'd hardly have to paint a solid line for miles when a dotted line or just a big blue X now and again would do. I know they like to paint things blue in old Mexico. They think it's a good-luck color, and they slop this sky-blue egg tempera over doorways, window frames, cantina tables and such until it looks mighty tedious. Only *ten miles* of it, on dry rock in dry country? I dunno, old son, that'd sure take the whites of many an egg, and mucho agua besides. Makes no sense, even for a greaser with a gold mine, holding money to be no object to his whims.''

Seth had to agree on that. He started to point out that running water could paint a streak at high water-level, against the slant of the rock layers, if something blue, mayhaps some natural mineral, was mixed with it. But he kept quiet. He knew old Elmo would just ask why in that case the mysterious streak only ran along *one* wall, and what melted in water to leave blue streaks but didn't just wash away in the next rain? They got more than ten inches of rain a year up here in the Hatchets, even on this dry side. The trees growing anywhere the soil ran deep enough for serious roots offered living proof of that.

They searched through the day without finding anything at all matching the old Indian's description. Late that afternoon, when they stumbled over a canyon offering both water and wood for their campfire, Elmo Dawson decided this was where he meant to camp and to hell with anyone else who knew about it.

Once they'd dismounted and began to set up, of course, Dawson naturally had second thoughts and decided to post lookouts in two-hour shifts on the rimrock above. Seth volunteered for first watch. He was no fool. He got to watch a glorious sunset whilst he avoided any camp chores down below.

As he did so, scanning the jagged black ridges against the molten-copper western skyline for movement, it seemed as if one bitty cloud to the west-southwest tumbleweeded north against the sunset more like dust or woodsmoke than moisture. He studied it hard for a spell, trying to picture how either dust or woodsmoke might have gotten there as he gauged the altitude of the already-vanishing whatever. A wagon trail or a column of field artillery might stir dust above the level of the surrounding rimrock. Smoke seemed more likely, assuming one hell of a fire built by someone too brave or dumb to care if they were giving themselves away or not. That sort of let an Indian war party out.

Seth had been twelve years old back east when George Armstrong Custer had made that wrong turn up by the Little Big Horn. But the papers coast to coast had been filled with speculation as to how an experienced Indian fighter like Old Yellow Hair could have ridden into an encampment of say a thousand lodges in broad daylight without noticing any smoke at all.

Seth smiled thinly as he lit a smoke up there for himself, making sure to cup his palms good around the match as he did so. It hadn't occurred to him until just this minute that the Custer fight had taken place about this time of the year, albeit neither the country nor the Indians involved had been exactly the same. Old Benny had said something about that, if only he could recall it.

Soon the mysterious, hazy cloud was only a memory. Seth's eyes were drawn more to the southwest as his ears detected a dull rumble. It sounded like distant thunder. Growing up as he had in the lee of the Wachung Mountains of New Jersey, Seth Grant considered himself an expert on summer thunderstorms, with good reason. North Jersey was the thunder capital of the east coast, if not the whole country. Only he'd yet to see summer lightning against a sky as clear and *dry* as this one. The so-called bolt from the blue did happen. Seth had almost caught one as a kid when it decided to hit that old oak instead. But even so, it had been a muggy, overcast evening. There had to be more going on in the sky than *this* to rate bolt one. Seth wet a finger and held it up to see if there was any shift in the air at all. There barely was. An almost undetectable breeze from the south accounted for the movements of that long-gone little cloud. But stare as he might, Seth couldn't spy anything else in the way of a cloud on the clear horizon. So when, almost an hour later, he heard that dull, distant boom a second time, he decided, "The army must be sort of exploring ahead with artillery. They'd be firing more and faster, if they knew they had a serious target."

Seth wondered if he ought to go down and warn the others a four-pound shell might be dropping in on them for dessert. He decided it could wait until he was relieved up here. Whether that was distant artillery or even farther dry lightning, there seemed to be no present danger. No present danger to his own party at least. It was hard not to feel sort of sorry for the intended targets of any casually lobbed shells, no matter what the papers printed about Geronimo. Benny had said his wilder kinsmen had more women and children tagging along than men. It sounded like a dumb way to fight. He wondered why some fighting men brought their whole damned families along. Then he remembered what he'd read in a book about the last days of the Roman Empire and how gents who lived for nothing but fighting, such as Celts, Gauls, Huns, and Bedoins kept their families with 'em on the march, because, otherwise, they'd never get to *see* their families worth mention.

As he tried to picture what it might be to live like that, he could see why even other Indians called Benny's folk Apache and other mean things. Poor old Benny had wanted to calm down and live more peaceable. He might have been able to in a white man's world where bullies like Hamp Ferris didn't abound. But Seth suspected that if it hadn't been Hamp old Benny had been forced to fight, it would have been another just as mean and mule-headed. Apache weren't the only ones who'd ever been taught it was more manly to be mean than decent or even smart.

A lot of folk, red and white, were just going to have to grow up before this old world could wind up as sensible as it ought to be.

The sun was long gone; the stars had come out so bright it looked as if you could scoop 'em into your hat if you really stretched. Somewhere in the night a coyote was complaining about the injustice of it all when Virgin Joe came scraping up the tilted sandstone to tell Seth there was still some coffee, as long as he admired it cold. Seth filled his relief in on the distant rumbles he'd heard earlier, agreed it might have been thunder or mayhaps a rockslide, and went down to put away a mess of beans and a little tepid coffee before turning in for half the night. They woke him around four A.M. to relieve Big Dipper since Dawson neither pulled guard nor did any other camp chores. By the time Seth was back down in the still-cold but no longer really gray dawn Pinto and Little Dipper had rustled up a fair breakfast for him. As he ate it, seated cross-legged with his back against one canyon wall, a beam from the ever-rising sun suddenly lanced through from the east to bathe their well-watered canyon in dazzle, the trickle down the middle dappling the stone walls with dancing spangles of reflected light. Seth stared a spell and washed down the last of his bread and beans before it suddenly struck him. He went over to where Elmo Dawson was sipping his third cup of coffee, and said, "I think that's it. See how flood water long ago carved that level groove along the cliff across the way? See how that stone crop's growing out of it, forming a sort of stripe up and down this canyon as far as you can see?"

Elmo Dawson stared dubiously at the skinny but solid line of cliffside greenery and swallowed before he snorted, and said, "I'll take your word on the name of them weeds, boy. But a blue stripe, painted up just one side of the canyon?"

Seth insisted, "Benny never said it was painted. You can see the running water cut the same sort of ledge to either side, only stone crop grows better on the sunny side, facing south, so . . ."

"So when did you study plants and rocks? And whilst you're at it, tell me that old Apache was color blind! He said *blue*, not *green*, bless his old eyes and my old ears."

Seth shook his head, and explained, "Stone crop's not a native American plant. It's an old-country weed as grows on bare stone as a thick crop, like so. That's how I know what it is and how come Indians who weren't used to it might have paid so much mind to it."

"It's still green. A bright salad green!" Dawson insisted.

Seth nodded, and said, "Some old-time folk from the old country eat stone crop as a salad plant. I've never noticed much taste to the stuff. I'm trying to explain why Benny might have called it blue instead of green. I was trying to learn his words for things, too, and to tell the truth they just don't look at this old world the way you and me might. I tried to pin him down on numbers, colors, and such. They have more words than we need for some things and use fewer words than us for others. They have one word as signifies the color of that turquoise charm he wore along with the color of the sky and the color of the grass. I'd say turquoise was a sort of blue-green or greenish-blue. But when I told him that, he just laughed and said I was picking nits since anyone could see what we called blue and green were just different shades of the same color."

"That's dumb," said Dawson, adding, "I told you Indians were odd. Imagine not being able to tell blue from green!"

Seth shrugged, and replied, "Benny was just as certain the bay you ride and the chestnut he was riding were two different colors entire and not different shades of brown, unless he was talking about a white man on one brown horse and an Indian on another. My point is that he saw things different than us and described them as best he could in a lingo that didn't quite fit his own view of the world.''

Seth sensed he might not be getting through to Dawson and let it go at, ''Look, do you want to give this odd stripe of an imported weed a try? Or do we just go on searching for that painted blue streak you have your mind set on until we run out of food, run into Geronimo, or whatever?''

Elmo Dawson grimaced, and replied, ''You do paint a cheersome picture, and I said before I couldn't see even a loco greaser expending that much egg tempera for no reason.''

He set his tin cup aside, got to his feet, and strode across the narrow canyon, leaping the rivulet of running water. Seth followed. On the far side Dawson plucked a spring of the succulent stone crop, tasted it, and decided, ''You're right about it not having much to offer. More water to it than anything. But just the same, it's a weed as goes with white folk, even greasers from Spain?''

Seth looked uncertain, and replied, ''I think so. The old lady who told me what it was, back home where she had some growing along her garden wall, said it had followed her and her kin across the main ocean, uninvited. She never said where in Europe they'd started out.''

Dawson decided, ''Mexican pack mules moving up and down this canyon many a year could have scattered all sorts of weeds along the way an Apache would find odd. You done right to tell me about your notion, old son. Even if you're wrong, it's worth a try. You were right about it only being a question of time afore we run out of supplies or into Apache!''

* * *

Seth's hunch had been right. The horizontal band of stone crop ran thick or thin a good six winding miles upstream, to the west, before a heavy rumble in the air and a tingle of the rocks all around them gave them pause near a sharp bend in the canyon. Elmo Dawson called back, "That was dynamite, not all that far. We'd best fort up and study some on this."

As Seth dismounted near their leader, Dawson added, "You'd best slither topside and see what you can bird's-eye for us up ahead, seeing you seem to think you know where in thunder you've been leading us."

Seth didn't say it was unfair. He knew it was, but he would have wanted to find out what was going on up ahead in any case. So he tethered his pony to some dwarf juniper growing from a rock cleft, slung his Winchester across his back, and commenced to work his way up the steep but not sheer canyon wall as the others took up more defensive positions behind boulders to either side of the crooked water course. He heard that same dull thud and felt the rocks he was clinging to kick like gun grips. Farther up the canyon a loose rock let go to clatter to the bottom. A couple of the boys below cussed hard, but when Seth looked down the falling boulder hadn't hit anything worth mention.

He rolled over the edge above and crawled higher up on the rooflike slope north of the canyon proper. When he made it to the heart-stopping drop-off running north and south he lay flatter still and gave a long, low whistle. He had a bird's-eye view indeed, and what he was looking at was a parklike valley, say half a mile across and running mostly green and grassy in line with the north-south ridges it nestled between. The same narrow stream they'd followed so far up that canyon ran down the center of the demi-Eden. Any trees along it had been long since cleared

away, albeit there were conifers growing in scattered
stands on the gentler rises that marked the western slope
of the valley. But the overall layout of the secluded dell,
attractive as it might be, paled in importance next to the
cluster of long, low structures and corrals. He had missed
seeing them at first because the obvious mine site

been thrown together further up the valley, against the
base of the cliffs he was peering over.

The notion someone had thrown together a mining camp
about where the old Indian had told them they'd find a
mine was not surprising. What was surprising were the
indications that the mine was back in operation, if it had
ever really been abandoned. The ponies in the corral beyond the sod-roofed structures of country rock and logs
could have belonged to most any breed. But the two gents
wheeling a crude mining tram wore the white cotton duds
and straw sombreros Seth had already learned to associate
with southwesterners of the Hispanic persuasion.

The two Mexicans ran the tram to the end of its wooden
tracks and left it there, near a big pile of what looked to
Seth like plain old railroad ballast. He heard and felt another dull dynamite blast and muttered, half-aloud,
"Right. First you bust a heap of ore out of the workface.
Then you muck it out to where you can get at it. Then you
work on it with water a spell before you have to blast any
more loose."

Seth reached absently for a smoke. Then he remembered where he was and what he was doing and decided
not to. Knowing the Mexicans below wouldn't be going
anywhere important for a spell, Seth studied the higher
country to see who might be coming. Those folk down
there had surely heard by now, there were two or more
bands of Apache out this summer. He knew there was no
way to mine gold from a hardrock vein without blasting,
but had he been in charge he'd have surely been blasting

at night, late at night, in hopes the exact location of his thumps and bumps could get sort of lost in the dark.

Of course, if those were the same Mexicans who'd found the mine to begin with, they likely figured the Apache already knew where the place was, having attacked there at least once in the past. That was something to study on. But having seen about all there was to see for now, Seth worked his way down to fill Elmo Dawson and the others in on the new game fate had dealt them.

Old Elmo looked so unhappy about it, Seth felt called upon to sort of apologize, saying, "I'd have been proud to tell you the old mine was still up for grabs, if those Mexicans hadn't beaten us back to it, if they ever left."

"God damn it, Benny told me his band didn't leave any!" protested Dawson. But Seth pointed out, "He told us neither he nor any of the others ever went down in the mine either. There's usually at least one shift working underground, and tell me something, would you come out an adit like a woodchuck with a mess of wild Indians dancing about up top?"

Little Dipper, who'd been listening, asked what an adit was. When Virgin Joe snorted, and said, "That's the way in or outten a mine shaft, you fool!" Little Dipper opined he'd never be foolish enough to volunteer for an Indian massacre. So Elmo Dawson nodded grimly, and announced, "Well, what's done is done, and that only goes to show it takes a white man to do things right."

To their credit some of the others looked as startled as Seth when Dawson added, "I reckon if we want them greasers massacred by Apache right we're just going to have to take up the chore from where old Benny and Loco left off."

Seth protested, "Hold on, you can't just attack those miners as if we were Apache ourselves!"

Dawson asked, "Why not? Who's going to stop us, old son?"

Seth knew it made more sense to just draw and be done with it than to defy openly a hardcase backed by five other gun hands. But it was likely safe to try. "We don't know how many of 'em there may be to begin with. From the open way they've been operating the mine, it's a safe guess they're not too worried about either Naiche nor Geronimo, and that's more than *I* can say right now."

He saw he'd scored a point with the others, and even Dawson looked less decided as he replied, "Yeah, it might be best to scout 'em afore we make our move. You speak Spanish, don't you, Wagner?"

Kid Wagner laughed, and said, "That was German you heard me cussing in that time, boss. Little Dipper here talks tolerable whorehouse Spanish, being from Texas and all."

The short Texan spat, and protested, "Talking to a good-looking greaser gal is one thing. Scouting her armed-and-dangerous brothers may be another thing entire! I ain't going near them fool Mexicans. Not by myself leastways. Mexicans who ain't afeared of Apache ain't about to fall down in a faint when they see little old me a-coming at 'em."

Dawson suggested, "Take Grant here with you." Then he turned to Seth to add, too sincerely, "You'd like to make sure none of us gets hurt, right?"

Seth started to say he didn't want anyone to get hurt if he could help it. He wasn't sure this was the time or place to say it. He turned to Little Dipper, and said, "Let's give her a try."

Little Dipper protested, "What if them greasers are just as bad as them Apache? What if they decide to gun us afore we can gun them?"

To which Seth Grant could only reply, "In that case you

and I won't have anything to worry about, while everyone else will be in a hell of a mess. Let's go."

Little Dipper wanted to move in along the base of the cliff to their right, the last furlong or so afoot so's they could duck for cover behind any number of boulders that had long since fallen from the rimrocks above. But Seth insisted they follow the stream up the open centerline of the valley for at least two good reasons. When he pointed out how sinister it might look to anyone watching strangers pussyfoot their way from one patch of cover to another, Little Dipper asked what his second reason might be. So Seth said, "Skulking behind a big rock works both ways. I'd rather have a sorehead meet me out in the open on even terms than I might to have him pop out of nowheres at me like an infernal jack-in-the-box."

They were already well on their way, walking their ponies along the east bank of the shallow stream by now. But Little Dipper still felt obliged to point out, "Giving them plenty of time to see us coming seems a sure way to give 'em lots of time to make up their minds about just how they ought to greet us."

Seth nodded soberly, and replied, "I just said that. That cheating stage-coach Jehu back to Deming never gave me time to consider various ways of dealing with his poor manners. Fights great and small are inclined to commence as much by accident as design. Even as we speak those Mex gents up ahead must have spotted us by now, and look how much time we're giving them to consider their options."

Little Dipper spat, and protested, "My dear old momma never raised her child to furnish target practice for morose Mexicans, damn it!"

Seth soothed, "They don't want to get shot any more than we do, and if they have a pair of eyes and a brain between 'em, they've already read us as likely scouts for a bigger outfit, coming in with pure hearts and repeating rifles as well as our sidearms. Aside from the simple risks of a stand-up fight on open ground, it's dumb as hell to declare war before you know who you're up against.''

Little Dipper pointed out, ''Old Elmo seemed ready to just ride in shooting, didn't he?''

To which Seth could only reply, ''I wish you'd pay attention and save me the trouble of repeating myself.''

By this time they were a little over halfway to the nearest outbuildings of the mine site. At first one, then two, then more like two dozen men and boys sporting white Mex work duds and Connecticut Yankee weaponry formed an informal skirmish line up ahead. Little Dipper gulped, and murmured, ''I see what you mean. Old Elmo might have been just a mite hasty after all.''

Seth didn't answer. He'd barely swung up-slope toward the miners and the property they seemed to be guarding before four Mexicans came unstuck to meet them halfway or more. Seth reined in as he noticed some of the less stable Mexicans farther up the slope were waving their guns sort of silly. He stopped just outside easy rifle range. Little Dipper did the same without asking why. That left the delegation coming down their way on foot with the odds in their favor a mere two to one. It didn't slow them worth mention. As they strode within conversational range the obvious leader of the Mexican quartet turned out to be a stocky individual with pockmarked Indian features. He could have been any age from thirty to fifty. Despite his squat build and bowlegs he walked as proud and prissy as a matador in the fancy green leather boots sticking out below his white cotton bell-bottoms. His buscadero gunrig was of tooled green leather as well. His two six-guns were silver-mounted Colt .45s. He let his three backups pack the long-guns, expensive bolt-action and clip-fed

Mannlichers that had only appeared on the market the year before. Seth had seen line cuts of them in a magazine article he'd read. Old Ritter von Mannlicher claimed his fancy Austro-Hungarian army rifles would carry flat the good part of a country mile. It was likely just a brag, but Seth knew this Mex outfit would have the range on Elmo and the boys if even half of 'em had been issued such fancy hardware.

Seth also knew there was a good chance the rascals were showing off the few good guns they had for the same reasons nobody told a gal he'd just met that he was out of a job. Little Dipper was tolerable at bluffing as well. He kept his voice calm and casual as he nodded at the boss Mex and began, "Buenos días, Señor. Enartar, nosotros . . ."

"I shall tell you for how to begin with!" The husky Hispanic cut in, his own English not really that much better than Little Dipper's Spanish, as he added, "To begin with you speak the language of my people like a pimp, and after that you speak it badly. We do not care who you are. All that is of importance to both sides is that you are going back the way you came if you wish for to go on living. You are already inside the boundry lines of the Robles Claim. If you wish to die right now, advance just one more foot!"

Seth said, "Let's not talk any sillier than we have to, neighbor. None of us is looking for trouble."

But the Mexican spat, "You are already in trouble. We are talking about the exact date of your death. We know what you are looking for. You are not the first claim jumpers we have had to deal with. Do you wish for to back off, or do you wish for to shoot it out? Is not so important to me and mine, but make up your gringo minds so we can get it over with, eh? We got more important work for to do around here than the swatting of flies."

Seth's carbine was already cocked with a round in the chamber. So he shifted its balance just enough to draw attention to the cocked hammer without being downright impolite as he softly replied, "Before anyone swats anything let's jaw some about the mineral claim you hold you're working up here, way off the officious map."

The burly Mexican shrugged, and growled, "Try for to take it away from me and my patron, and you shall see we need no gringo paper for to defend his rights against any number of gringo gold grabbers. But I may as well warn you that even if you beat us by some miracle, you would be in trouble with your own gringo government. Don Robles got the damned mining permit from Tío Sam if you try to say his grants from both El Rey y La Republica de Mejico don't count no more, eh?"

Little Dipper protested, "Hold on, we was told you boys was dead to begin with and squatter-miners afore that!"

Seth sensed from the Mex leader's frown that Little Dipper might have put that in a more diplomatic fashion. He hushed the Texan with a warning look and told the segundo or whatever, "What my pard meant was that Apache run over some other Spanish gents digging gold up here a few years back with nothing down on paper in English. Is it safe to say Mr. Donald Robles is another gent entire with a proper mineral claim recorded with the proper U.S. authorities?"

The burly Mexican grimaced, and said, "Now you are buzzing in circles, little fly. I told you I got more important work to do. If you wish for to dispute my right to work or even my right for to spit in your mother's milk, let us see you try!"

Before things could get much worse one of the other Mexicans called softly, "Mirar, Gordo, la heredara." Seth didn't need to speak Spanish to see they were talking about a gal headed their way aboard a copper-colored barb as proud-looking and almost as pretty as she was. The gal's black riding outfit and flat black hat looked Spanish as did her mount, and the mining men whipped off their hats at her approach. But as Seth looked more closely things got less certain. For the features of the pretty gal riding at them sidesaddle were as North European as any Yankee gal might manage, and her hair was the same shade of burnished copper as her mount's shiny hide. She carried a rustic riding crop of braided rawhide and had a gun belt strapped about her trim waist. Her big old Starr .45 rode cross-draw on her left hip, much easier to draw in a side-saddle position. She called out to the burly Gordo in their own lingo. You didn't have to speak Spanish to figure out what "Los Indios de Geronimo" might mean. Still, Little Dipper leaned closer to confide in a low tone, "The gal says this is no time for Christian folk to be fighting each other with you-know-who fixing to pop over the skyline any minute."

Gordo rattled back at his apparent boss-lady too fast for Little Dipper to follow. As she joined them with a polite but sort of frosty smile she switched to English, better English than Gordo or for that matter Seth could manage, saying, "There is at least one band of Apache, maybe more, perhaps a day's ride to the north. How many guns ride with the two of you, señores?"

Before Seth could decide just how truthful he wanted to be, the Mexican standing his ground between the three horses snorted in overdramatic disgust and announced in English for all who understood the same to hear, "Apache are the least of our problems, mi patrona! Apache care nothing for mining and these claim-jumping ladrones were just asking about your padre's Yanqui papers!"

The imperious Spanish beauty stared incredulously at Seth, and told him, "If it wasn't such a ridiculous matter to discuss now, I could show you our family mining claims, as they have been registered in both Ciudad Mejico y Santa Fe and even Deming, I think. But do you not agree our mutual survival seems more important at a time like this?''

Seth agreed, but Gordo shook his head stubbornly and insisted, ''Let me rid you of these pests, Doña Felicidad! If either Naiche or Geronimo are really off the San Carlos Agency as some say, we still have the Espina de la Cordillera between us and Fort Bowie. So even should those bare-legged pobrecitos get past los soldados Yanqui on the far side, for why would they wish to come over on our side through the icy winds of the few passes, eh?''

She sat her mount even straighter to reply in a tone of dismissal, ''I was just telling our visitors this seems an estupido time for to split hairs! Do you expect me to tell you why Apache do the odd things they do or even what they might do next? The continental divide did not keep them away from this very valley the time they came over that very lomo to the west to murder my Tío Pablo and most of the others here, did it?''

Gordo looked uncomfortable, and said, ''Was not the same, Doña Felicidad. The one called Loco was well named. There were many more bands out and not as many soldados chasing them that time. Geronimo is not just out for blood like Loco was. For why should he come over on this side of la Cordillera when the wastelands of Sonora are so much easier for to get to?''

Before the boss lady could agree with her segundo, Seth cut in. ''For openers the Mexican Army's no doubt watching the border with at least as much interest as our own. Aside from that, I just met up with an Indian scout called Tom Horn betwixt here and Deming. He said he was scouting for them Apache on this side of the continental divide, and if he's wrong, the U.S. Cavalry's lost for sure this summer.''

The copper-haired gal nodded soberly, and murmured, ''I asked how many guns you ride with, Señor.''

Before Seth could answer Gordo glared past him down the valley, yelling, ''Five more at least, mi patrona! And here they come without permiso! So with all due respect . . .''

''Hold your fire, and peel your eyes to your right!'' Seth yelled as he pointed his Winchester at the bitty white cloud rising oddly lonesome against the otherwise clear afternoon sky. Gordo gasped, and grudgingly added, ''Ay caramba!'' as another smoke puff followed the first above the timber-covered ridge to their west. As Seth twisted in his saddle to regard old Elmo and the others making their way posthaste, he stated flatly, ''That ain't no cavalry charge, ma'am. Our pals can see them smoke signals as well as we can, and it's safe to assume they ain't being sent from up yonder by any pals of your'n or mine!''

Felicidad Robles raised her riding crop to wave Elmo and the others on in faster as she called out, ''Vamanos! Muy pronto! First we get everyone on our side behind something bulletproof. Then we argue about less important matters such as gold mines, eh?''

As he rode closer to the bossy little thing Seth asked her if that had meant she considered them on the same side. She wasn't smiling as she answered, ''Against Apache? Right now I'd consider the Grand Mufti of the Turks a comrade, if he was here. For I know if he was, he'd fight those fiends from hell side by side with us.''

As she whipped her barb to a faster pace she added, ''Everyone fights Apache as hard as they can. You see, the Apache give one no choice in the matter at all!''

* * *

Elmo Dawson and the segundo or straw boss called Gordo claimed to have tangled with Apache before. So once they finished sniffing at one another like growly dogs who'd just met while hunting the same varmin, they agreed the so-called smoke signals on the ridge to their west was an old Indian dodge meant to spook them, distract them, or both. Gordo opined and Elmo agreed the Apache would want to scout them good, mayhaps with some otherwise pointless powwow, before moving in under cover of darkness, if they tried at all. This time it was Gordo's turn to agree when Elmo suggested the Indians were more interested in picking up more weapons, ammo, and ponies than they were the gold or even the women. When Seth said he'd heard Indians didn't like to attack at night, lest their spirits get lost in the dark if they were killed, both older men favored him with disgusted looks. Elmo was too polite to call him what Gordo did in Spanish. Elmo said, "Forget anything you may have read in penny dreadfuls about Buffalo Bill, old son. If there be any hostiles as wouldn't rather creep in on you in the dark I've yet to meet 'em. As for Apache in particular, it's about the only time they ever attack, once they know you know they're there. Apache don't hold with heroics. They consider it dumb as hell to die for their cause when they can make you die for your own. They don't make war as we or even the Sioux understand the subject. The name of their game is dirty. The dirtier the better. So just do as this dirty greaser and I say, and you just might come outten this fix alive."

That shut Seth up about as well as it was doubtless intended to. He left the two self-appointed strategists to sort out the defense of the mining camp and drifted off to satisfy his own curiosity as to just what they had to defend and what they might have to work with. Nobody paid much attention to one harmless-looking youth as they busied themselves with their own chores or, failing that, did a heap of praying with those rosary beads Mex papists packed.

In addition to the seven well-armed Americans and Gordo's two dozen riflemen, there were another eight or ten Mexican workmen and eighteen or twenty women, half of them pretty, who seemed to be there as dependents of the mining men or house servants of Felicidad and her father. He also counted a dozen odd little kids that went with the mining men and their mujeres. Felicidad let him into a separate cabin and introduced him to the skinny old man who lay in bed under quilts, despite the heat. Don Hernan, as he was called, barely managed to open one eye and sort of breathe a mite harder when they were introduced.

Seth felt no call to argue when the mine owner's daughter led him back out on their veranda, murmuring something about her old man coming down with an ague he'd caught years before in some swamp. Seth got out a cheroot with a questioning glance. When she nodded, he lit up before he indicated the long but gentle slope across the valley, and told her, "Elmo says they're not likely to charge down all that open ground at us, by moon or sunlight. Trying to think mean and sneaky as some say Apache like to fight, I've been studying the steeper cliffs rising above us on this side of the creek."

She nodded and said, "They can't roll boulders off the rimrocks this time. They used up all the loose rock up there the last time they attacked and, in any case, only the adit itself is within range of a boulder rolling over the edge from above. Survivors of the last attack told us the ones above ground were overrun late at night. The ones who were hiding in the mine shaft at the time did not take part in those last mad moments, of course, so it is not too clear how the Indians got the upper hand in the end."

Seth sighed, and said, "The one old Indian who might

have been able to tell us can't now. Since we don't seem to be up against the same band, they might try it another way this time. That was dynamite you folk were setting off earlier today, wasn't it?''

She said, ''Of course. Is that how you found your way here, by the sounds of our blasting down below?''

He nodded soberly, and replied, ''I doubt we were the only ones who might have been attracted by the noise. But let's not argue about how dumb it was to rattle the hills with Apache nearby, now that they're even closer. The question left before the house is how much dynamite do we still have to work with?''

She shrugged, and told him, ''Enough for between now and let us say the first frost and time to quit for the year. Why do you ask? Surely we can't spare any of the men at the ore face with Apache about to attack! Mi padre, I mean my father, brought enough guns, good guns, for even the women to fire back at those red demons this time, and . . .''

''They're not likely to offer themselves as targets for even unskilled marksmen,'' he cut in, adding, ''Coming in from the south just now, that Texas cowboy I was with suggested moving from one big boulder to the next along the base of the cliffs. To tell the truth I was tempted. I decided it looked more innocent, in broad daylight, to approach the way we did. Had it been dark, with the moon rising to the east and them cliffs casting ink-black shade halfway across this valley . . .''

''Madre de Dios!'' she gasped, making the sign of the cross as he nodded grimly and continued, ''It might not work as good as it sounds, given some preparations on our part. When you blast down in your gold mine do you use old-timey match-lit fuses or the new electricated kind, ma'am?''

When she assured him her father had re-opened the mine with up-to-date blasting gear for the same reasons he'd purchased the most modern rifles on the market, Seth smiled sort of wolfishly, and said, "I was hoping you'd say that, Miss Felicidad. Do I have your permit to ask Gordo for all the dynamite, fuse wire, and battery plungers I might require?"

She said simply, "Gordo has nothing to say about such matters. *I* do, as long as I must act in my father's name. Are you suggesting we rig those boulders along the base of the cliffs to blow up in Apache faces?"

He shook his head soberly, and said, "I'm not suggesting anyone but me ought to wire them rocks, Miss Felicidad. I don't know beans about mining gold, and I'd be fibbing if I bragged on being an old Indian fighter. But back home in Essex County we had more stumps to clear and rocks to shatter than I like to look back on. So I got to know a thing or two about making noise. You blast stumps with black powder because black powder pushes, sort of like high-pressure steam, and you want your stump flying out of the ground in one hunk. But you blast old plow-busting boulders with dynamite, because dynamite shatters stuff without moving it all that far."

She grinned, most likely picturing Apache shattered to mighty messy shards. She said, "Bueno. I shall see you have all the dynamite and detonating wire you need. But how do you expect to see Apache behind boulders in the dark? This is my first summer up here, but this will not be my first dark night in these mountains, and you were right about the inky shadows the moon casts until midnight or even later, Señor."

He said, "Call me Seth, Miss Felicidad. I ain't that much senior to you, and as for illuminating Apache, I'm still working on that. You can only eat an apple a bite at a time. So I'd best worry about how I'll see 'em after I'm set up to blast 'em."

She agreed that made sense, sort of, and allowed she'd

show him to their explosives shed, which was naturally set up, sandbagged, behind the gentle rise just north of the corrals. But they'd just made it down off her veranda when a young Mex boy came running, excited and breathless, to yell at her in their own lingo. Seth only caught "caballero" meaning a rider and "Apache" meaning just what it sounded like. But it was enough so he wasn't too surprised when Felicidad turned to him to say, "The Indians seem to be sending in a messenger. Your patron, the one called Elmo, thinks it would be best if the Apache saw as many armed hombres as possible."

Seth said that made sense, and the three of them circled to move in behind the mess hall cum cantina that was big enough to look halfway impressive. The Mex kid opened the back door for them. As Felicidad led the way through, Seth spotted a crate of rifles near the front door and said, "Hold on. Let's all three of us join the fun and games looking armed and dangerous."

The lady who really owned all the hardware just smiled like a mean little kid as Seth handed her a bolt-action military rifle. The young Mexican boy laughed out loud when he was given one to play with, too. Seth asked Felicidad to warn him not to fool with the bolt like that lest anyone else notice he didn't know beans about bolt actions. She had the boy toting his dangerous-looking weapon more seriously as they stepped out on the front veranda to join Gordo, Elmo, and some of the others. All packed the same new Mannlichers. Seth nodded approvingly. Then he spied the lone Indian walking his paint pony way down the far slope and softly asked Elmo, "Might the way he's got his fool face painted mean anything?"

Elmo shrugged, and said, "Hard to say with his breed. You saw how Benny killed Hamp Ferris with no paint worth mention on his sweet old face. Afore he went so hostile himself, Benny told me one time that they mostly wear that white stripe across their faces to tell friend from foe in a night fight.''

Seth studied the oncoming envoy with his eyes squinted almost shut. Then he nodded, and said, ''Makes sense. The white stripe on a skunk stands out in dim light, too. I don't think skunks have any friends, but them distinct stripes might save both them and, say, a hungry bobcat an embarrassing accident in tricky light.''

The Indian on the paint pony had ridden close enough for the soft sounds of his monotonous chanting to reach them. As the Indian forded the stream, Little Dipper asked why the fool Indian was singing like so.

Seth was mildly surprised when Felicidad of all people explained that the Déné, as she called him, was chanting his death song, most likely to show them he was not afraid to die. She added, ''Half our workers are as Indio as he is, albeit from more reasonable razas, and so they know what he is up to, and he knows they know, and so forth.''

Gordo growled something in Spanish that sounded urgent as well as respectful at the same time. Felicidad demurely replied, ''Pero ciertamente! Comprendo perfectamente.'' She explained to Seth before he could ask, ''Gordo was worried about my speaking out of turn, since my interest in Los Indios is well known. One would have to be most ignorant of that one's customs to speak first to him, when one happens to be as inferior a being as Santa Maria, Madre de Dios!''

''You mean Apache don't talk to ladies?'' Seth asked.

She shrugged, and replied, ''They must on occasion, or they'd have surely died out by this time. But one gets the impression they regard women as livestock to be stolen and, ah, mastered as casually as one begs, borrows, or steals a pony. They never *buy* either, if they can possibly help it. Property must be obtained by force as a tribute, if it is to be worth boasting about."

Seth said he could see Apache liked to brag some as the one on the paint horse reined in at oration range to bang his fool self in the head with the barrel of his Spencer repeater and lard his Spanish sermon with so much "Yo" and "Me." Seth had figured out that Yo meant the same as I in Spanish, and any fool could see what Me meant. Felicidad murmured, "He says he is not afraid to fight all you men at once, bare-handed, and you shall just have to guess what he says he would like to do to me and all the other women in camp, again all at once."

"That's sort of hard to picture," said Seth dryly. She looked away with her cheeks a pretty shade of pink as she insisted they stick to the Indian's droll notions, adding, "Now he says that even though he has the heart of Real Bear and the cunning of Coyote, he and his people are misunderstood by our kind."

"He lumps your folk with mine?"

"Not really. They hate Mexicans worse, but he doesn't know we know this, or perhaps he seeks to flatter us by pretending he thinks all of us are Yanqui. In either case he says he and his people are being persecuted for no reason by your army. He says they only wish to be Déné again, at peace with all others, as long as they are free to hunt and fish as they please in the lands Spider Woman led their ancestors to, long, long ago in the Grandfather Time and . . ."

"Apache don't eat fish," Seth cut in, explaining, "A friendly Apache told me this, personal."

She shrugged and replied, "I never told you this one was telling the truth, did I? He says his band only left the San Carlos Agency to gather pinyon nuts in the Gila Mountains, and the next thing they knew the army was after them with field guns."

Seth protested, "The papers say they commenced the festivities this spring by hitting an Arizona homestead and butchering everything on the property but the ponies and one young gal they seem to have carried off."

Felicidad hushed him with, "I just said he was lying. The Gila Mountains are *on* the big San Carlos Agency, and even if they weren't, you don't gather pinyon nuts in the spring. Oh, here it comes, he's saying his chief just wants to camp further up the valley to be safe from the cruel bluesleeves, and that we have their word they won't bother us if only we'll be good neighbors and be kind to those less fortunate."

"You mean he's actually begging for . . . what?"

"Anything he can get, I suppose. I told you it was only a disgrace when one had to admit one had *paid* for something."

Felicidad touched Seth's sleeve for silence as the Apache envoy went on in a whining tone of sweet reason. She told Seth, "Here it comes. He says his band will know we are friends who won't give them away to the government if we hand them presents. He says guns and ammunition are always welcome, but he's waiting to see what Gordo might wish for to offer."

Gordo had obviously been expecting some such speech in advance. He simply snapped his fingers and, a peon kid came forward with two brown liquor jugs. Seth assumed from the corncob stoppers that they were filled with some Mexican home brew. The Apache must have, too. He asked Gordo dubiously, "Es tiswin?" to be soothingly assured by the grinning Gordo that it was better than tiswin or Apache moonshine. Before their visitor could say one way or the other Gordo had the kid jog nervously out to the Indian with the jugs. Seth wondered just how the Apache was going to manage. Then he saw the Indian had dealt with jugs great and small before. All the Apache had to do was run the ends of his reins through the jug handles, and they made a fairly neat load betwixt his thighs on the hornless officer's flat saddle the cuss had begged, borrowed, or most likely stolen along with the pony. Slinging his Spencer to have both hands free to juggle the jugs, the Apache grudgingly told Gordo he'd see what else his chief might want after they'd seen how good this tiswin was. Then he pulled a corncob with his teeth to sample one of the jugs as he swung his pony's broad rump toward them to ride grandly back the way he'd come. As the Indian raised the jug to drink in the rustic drunk's way, riding his right elbow, Gordo cursed, and said, "Pero no, tonto! En campo, no aquí!"

Seth never guessed how much Gordo meant his words until Felicidad demanded in English, "What did you just give that Déné, Gordo?"

Gordo only had time to confess sheepishly, "Just a little coyote bait, Doña Felicidad." Before the Indian had made it to the far side of the stream, he let out an awesome wail and cartwheeled off his pony in a rigid spread-eagle as if nailed to a St. Andrews cross. Then he landed on his face, his spine arched like a fully drawn bow, to rock in that same grotesque position on his belly, spewing vomit and mindless screams, as Elmo Dawson decided, "That has to be nux vomica you fed that Apache, pard. How'd you hide the taste, strong as that dosage has to have been?"

Gordo confessed modestly, "Was easy. The mescal in those jugs was vile for to begin with. Pero was not my plan for the greedy pig to drink ahead of the rest of his band, like so."

As the poisoned Indian writhed in agony out in plain view of both sides Felicidad swore at her segundo in a most unladylike way and demanded to know how they'd ever gain the Indian's trust again now.

Even Seth had to allow Gordo had a point when he

replied with a fatalistic shrug, "They meant a war to the death before they got here, Doña Felicidad. Only difference now is that we got one less to worry about, and both sides can forget the usual flirting and get right down to business, no?"

Felicidad's reply was to demand a rifle round for her otherwise useless Mannlicher. When one of the Mexicans on the veranda handed her a round from his cartridge belt she worked the bolt of her rifle as if she'd already practiced some, inserted the round to load and lock, then simply raised it to draw a bead on the writhing Apache a good two hundred yards away. She fired, even as Gordo gasped, "Pero no! Should you miss . . ."

But she didn't. The Indian convulsing in spine-wrenching agony was put out of his misery for good, albeit in a sort of messy way, as Felicidad's well-aimed military round blew blood, brain tissue, and wisps of long black hair out the far side of his screaming head. As the trembling, rigid limbs of the poison victim went dishrag limp and deathly still, Felicidad said quietly, "Now we can get down to business, in the time we have left. To begin with I wish that pobrecito buried, on the far side but properly. He might have been a Christian, like they say Geronimo is."

Gordo shrugged, and said, "We'll get rid of him for you, mi patrona. But if Geronimo is a Christian I'm the czar of all the Russians, and need I say how they mean to treat *our* bodies, should they win?"

Since everyone kept saying it was time to get down to business and since the Apache had died not all that long before suppertime back home, Seth Grant had been busy as a beaver along the base of the cliff long before Felicidad caught up with him. She climbed on the rimrocks above the camp in time to watch the sunset with him from up there.

Getting to the top, even with another box of DuPont 60% and the gear to set it off with, had been easy enough once the kids who'd helped him down below had shown him the sort of natural stairwell running along the steep but not really vertical cliffs. Felicidad had made it up even easier, having nothing to pack along but that long-range rifle she seemed to have grown so fond of.

As she joined him atop a vast sandstone slab sloping gently east, away from the drop, she found him seated cross-legged behind a waist-high rock about the size and shape of a wagon bed with his own rifle and a somewhat-misnamed battery box—actually a pile of permanent magnets that heaved a sudden sigh of high voltage should one move another magnet of reversed polarity through them with the plunger sticking out the top of the wooden casing. As she crawled out of the cleft to join him there, he nodded, and said, "I was hoping someone would show up with a match. I got everything I need up here but a way to light the swell cigars old Elmo gave me for being so smart."

The Mexican girl fumbled in the pockets of her bolero jacket for matches as she answered in a puzzled tone, "They told me down below that you'd planted lots of dynamite charges along the cliff base. But what are we doing up here if you expect the Déné to move in from boulder to boulder down below?"

As she handed him the bitty box of wax-stemmed Mexican matches she'd found, Seth indicated a sort of Gordian knot of fuse wires wedged between the battery box and the big, square rock they reclined behind in the soft gloaming light. He explained, "I got the different wires coded with stripped insulation tied around each in a different way, figuring I'll never have to set anything off in light bright as this.''

He lit one of the cigars he'd brought along for company before he told her, "If I need to feed juice down one wire or another, I just have to touch it by feel to this feeder from the box, pump the plunger hard, and, Lord willing, set off the charge as needs to be set off.''

Being a miner's daughter, Felicidad hardly needed to have a battery box and fuse wires explained to her. But she still glanced thoughtfully at the bloodred sky to the west as she insisted, "You won't be able to make out anything moving along the base of the cliffs from up here on the rimrock, Seth. It would be difícil if you were posted down below, behind your own boulder, right?''

He said, "Wrong. There's no way to see both approaches from any one spot down there. Even if there was, the Indians are just as likely to crawl up this old hogback to fire over the edge.''

He took a thoughtful drag on his cigar before he added, "That's how I'd do her, if I was Geronimo. Given command of this high ground, I'd keep everyone below inside the mine or the buildings whilst I sent me some raiders down yonder slot we both climbed up.''

She stared wide-eyed at him, and decided, "Madre de Díos, that is the way *I* would do it, too, now that you have pointed out the obvious! But what are you doing up here *alone* if you expect the main attack across the bare rock all about us?''

He told her soothingly, "I never said they had to move in that way. I said they might. I've never been in a war before, but I used to read a lot about such adventurous doings betwixt farm chores, and one thing I noticed was that all the famous generals, like Napoleon or say Geronimo, try to avoid the tricks others expect 'em to pull. For all we really know they'll just charge down that gentle west slope at us, afoot or aboard their ponies, in which case Elmo, Gordo, and the others will surely dust 'em good with rifle fire by the light of the silversome moon. If they pussyfoot up or down the valley in the shade of these rimrocks the rocks down there I wired strategic ought to unsettle 'em some. They can't afford many more causalities than we can and . . . anyways, recalling what George Washington said about taking the high ground when you don't know what else to do, I asked some of the other boys to join me up here as soon as they're done with their other chores and fill up good on coffee. I figure betwixt me, the two dippers, and Kid Wagner, we can hold this position pretty good against redskins playing lizardbelly across all that open sandstone, don't you?''

Felicidad sat up straighter to lay her rifle atop the flat boulder, as she grimly regarded the few others of similar size and shape within rifle range. She said, ''It's not completely open up here, Seth. I count six . . . no, make that seven other rocks big enough to hide at least one hombre, most uncomfortably close!''

Seth chuckled dryly, and said, ''If you'd only look a mite harder, you'd see the wires I've strung from here to every one of 'em as well. Lucky for us, Loco's band must have rolled all the stuff they could move over the edge that last time they rid this way. But as soon as I saw them other immovable objects, I figured I'd best place charges under 'em.''

Felicidad gave off delighted sounds as she traced the almost-invisible, tar-coated wires across the edge-lit red sandstone. She still wanted to know where the dynamite might be, so he explained. ''Jammed under, anywhere's I could get it to go, of course. As you must know by now, dynamite's just nitroglycerin mish-mashed with a sort of clay to make it safer to handle. If you just bust open the pasteboard wrapper of a dynamite stick you can munch

the gooey stuff into any old hole or crevice. So that's what
I done to all them other rock slabs out yonder. I only had
to jam the wired caps into the goo once I had a few pounds
of bang-bang in place, and do we get us a sucker or more,
well, we'll see how my notion works.''

She clapped her hands like a gal-child who'd just spied
a lit-up birthday cake, and said, ''It *has* to work! That
grand a charge ought to shatter any of those other boulders
and anyone hiding behind! But how do you expect to know
when it is time to blow one up? I have been up on these
rock spines by moonlight. It is a good way to feel muy
muy nervoso, even when the moon is shining bright.''

She glanced at the deep purple sky to their east as she
licked her lips, and added, ''The moon shall rise full, it's
true, later tonight. Pero *mucho* later, Seth. No earlier than,
let us say, ten or eleven, and before that it promises to be
muy muy obscuro, no?''

He chuckled fondly, and said, ''I sure find it painless,
learning Spanish from you. I read this book by an English
explorer called Burton one time. He translated the Ara-
bian Nights from A-rab after learning the lingo with the
help of a pretty A-rab gal he called his horizontal dictio-
nary in his sarcasticated English way.''

Felicidad, red faced, warned him to stick to the subject
of a possible Indian attack. So he nodded, and said, ''I
may have rigged me a clever invention, and I may have
just wasted some of your dad's supplies I found whilst I
was grubbing about in your explosives shed. I'd feel better
if I had more eyes up here right now. For it's getting darker
by the minute, and I'd say you were right about that moonrise. When you get to the bottom you might ask old Elmo
why those other boys ain't up here, yet. Kid Wagner said
something about sandbagging walls down below, and if
Elmo has 'em tied up . . .''

She cut in to tell him, ''I'm not leaving you up here

alone with darkness and quíen sábe how many Déné creeping up that slope at us!''

He said he sure wished she would, and when that didn't work, he sighed, and said, ''Well, you do shoot a rifle better than half the men I know, and with any luck Kid Wagner and the two dippers ought to show up well ahead of . . . which band do you figure, Naiche or Geronimo?''

She shrugged, and said it could be either, neither, or both, explaining, ''The elders who had more control over such matters must be as disgusted as we are with los malos such as we are no doubt dealing with so late in the game. Naiche may just be in bad company, pero Geronimo, or Goyalka as true Christians of either race should call him, is the two-faced prince of renegades.''

Seth set his Stetson atop the rock between their long guns as he asked reflectively just what folk out this way meant when they called an Indian a renegade. He said he understood how the government might classify an Indian full of fight a hostile and a reasonable one a friendly, but added, ''As I understand the word, a renegade is a cuss who turns against his own kind. So how could even Geronimo or, all right, Goyalka . . .''

''He reneged on his own word, or broke a signed and sworn-to treaty,'' she cut in, adding, ''To begin with his own high chief, Cochise, made peace back in '73 in exchange for the right to go on living much the same over near San Carlos, save for the government allotments in cash and supplies he demanded for his people and got our government to agree.''

''*Our* government, Miss Felicidad?'' Seth asked without thinking.

She replied stiffly, ''Since the treaty of 1848 ceded New Mexico and everyone in it to Tío Sam, long before either of us could have been born, my family has been as gringo as your own, whether either of us like that or not.''

He soothed, "Us Yanks got to stick together, and you were telling me what makes some other folk renegades, remember?"

She smiled thinly, and explained, "Some others didn't agree to the peace treaty Cochise and more important leaders signed. Victorio, Nana, and others leading Mescalero instead of Chiricahua bands never thought the treaty applied to them to begin with."

"But Goyalka *was* Chiricahua," Seth pointed out.

It was not a question. But Felicidad still answered, "Baptized Geronimo at a Spanish mission as well. So his self-serving protestations every time he surrenders are no more than the whimpering lies of a captured thief. He was taught right from wrong by the padres long ago, yet every time the army corners him . . ."

"Hold on, how many time are we talking about?" Seth cut in.

She shrugged, and said, "Quíen sabe? He goes on the warpath every time he can entice a handful of malcontents to follow him." She frowned in thought, and added, "He was out with Loco from '82 to '83. General Crook cornered them, and they asked terms, with the Déné speaking scout, Al Sieber, translating for both sides. The terms were most generous when one considers how some Anglo and Mexican victims fared, including my uncle and a couple of female cousins Loco's band ran over in this very valley."

Seth said he'd heard about Al Sieber and told her what Tom Horn had said about Sieber's own Indians turning on him.

Felicidad didn't seem surprised. She said, "You must understand that while most Indios understand a promise as well as we do, even those Déné we now call Navaho, the ones who have insisted on remaining Apache, or Enemies, consider treachery and broken promises no more

than another way for to win. In '85, despite their promises
of '83, they were out again. So again the army tracked
them down, and after they'd raided in Old Mexico as well,
they had Los Federales chasing them, too. After a most
confusing affair in which Mexicans killed an Americano
officer named Crawford, most of the chiefs agreed to come
back in. Naiche and Goyalka, how you say, stalled?''

Seth nodded and thought he was agreeing when he said,
''So that's how come those two bands are still raising
hell.''

She shook her head, and replied, ''Pero no. Last pri-
mavera, General Crook held a grand peace meeting with
plenty of food and firewater. After three days of fiesta
everyone agreed to return to San Carlos. Most of them
did. The terms were most generous when one considers
how the government views bandits of your race or mine.
Pero, as we know, Goyalka broke his word again and,
with Naiche, slipped away to go on raiding.''

Seth turned to stare wistfully at the last rays of sunset
as he assured her he'd never ask what a renegade Indian
might be again. Then he said, ''Speaking of such redskins, it's almost dark, and so where in thunder could
those other boys be?''

She peered the other way, down-slope into the gathering darkness, as she complained, ''I can't see as far as the
chaparral from where this bare rock begins now. I can't
even make out the outlines of the more distant boulders
down the slope!''

He muttered, ''I just said that. Why don't you slide
down the cliff and tell them other boys to shake some
legs?''

She protested, ''Leaving you alone up here, in the
dark?''

He said, ''Aw, it ain't that dark when you're as scientificated as me. Hold on, I'll show you another stunt I've rigged up.''

She watched with interest as he touched one loose wire from his bundle to the lead from the battery box. He had to hold them together with his bare left thumb and forefinger. So it tingled some as he worked the plunger. But the real surprise to both of them, since he hadn't tried it before, was the way the darkness on the far side of their boulder gave way to a short but amazingly bright burst of artificial daylight.

As the light winked off just as suddenly Felicidad gasped, ''Mirar! Indios!'' and grabbed for her rifle.

He snapped, ''Don't! I saw 'em. Only two and way down the slope ahint another rock. So just sit tight, and we'll see what other wonders we can show the rascals.''

He was working almost completely by feel now, recalling the right wire by the insulation knotted around it as he concentrated on just which knots went with which boulders. If he was confused about the rocks those two blurs had crabbed behind in the split second of illumination, or if they'd moved up to the next boulder in the darkness, since . . .

But the longer he worried the longer he gave them. So he just held the infernal wires tightly together, shoved the plunger hard, and, as the not-so-distant dynamite went off, all hell busted loose.

The explosion twanged the solid rock under them like a hammer-struck saw blade, while flying rock from good-sized chunks to mighty fine sand rained down to tingle their world more. Felicidad made the sign of the cross, and gasped, ''Madre de Díos!'' as Seth changed contacts and sent a surge of power to his Edison bulb again.

In the short but brilliant flash of light that resulted they could both make out two bloody figures down beyond the shattered boulder they'd been crouched behind. As the light winked off again, a gun muzzle flashed from behind another boulder down that way. The bullet glanced off their shelter to go banshee-screaming through the night. Seth growled, "All right boys, seeing you still want to play, and seeing I got that rock wired as well . . ."

This time the noise was worse, the second boulder he was blowing being a mite closer. The next time he flashed light on the subject Felicidad gagged, and said, "Ay que sangriento!" He followed her drift enough to agree.

"Yep, that's one good Indian with a really red skin, what the dynamite left of it anyways."

She asked how he did that trick with the light. He explained, "You just said yourself it got dark around here after sundown. So once I had my charges placed, I had to consider how I'd be able to see what needed blasting. I knew any oil lamps I set out would only draw rifle fire from further out than its feeble rays could reach. You just heard that one cuss fire at the Edison bulb I rigged on the far side of this rock, short a flash as he had to aim at."

She laughed uncertainly, and said, "I recall those silly light bulbs someone put among our supplies, of course. I was most annoyed when we unpacked them, knowing we had no electric generating plant up here in these mountains."

He nodded, and said, "I was wondering what they could be doing amid your other supplies. But seeing they were there, and seeing you'd said I could help myself, it was easy enough to rig one shining down the slope as you just witnessed. I have others hanging over the edge of the cliff to wink on and off from time to time. Only I need more eyes than you and me have betwixt us if we're to discourage sneaks moving in from all directions. So be a good gal and scoot down to fetch those boys I told you about before the other side recovers from the surprise we just now gave 'em, eh?"

She might have. But then Kid Wagner crawled out of the nearby cleft to shout, "Elmo wants to know what all that infernal blasting was about."

Seth replied, "Get over here and we'll show you."

But Seth wasn't really expecting to see any Indians alive and well when he gripped the right leads together and fed some juice to that Edison bulb. So it was Felicidad who fired her high-powered rifle just as Seth's first flash winked out, and when he flashed again, sure enough, a fourth Indian lay writhing on the rock near the more torn-up body he'd been trying to haul away in the darkness. The three or four who'd been with him had vanished entire.

Kid Wagner whistled in wonder, and chortled, "I swear you're as tricksome as Tom Edison and Old Nick put together!" Then he told Felicidad, "You shoot good, too, ma'am."

She thanked him, and told Seth, "I think the ones I missed dropped behind that wedge-shaped rock just to the left of the one I just hit."

Seth nodded, and said, "It looked that way to me, too. Let's find out." Then he shoved the plunger down to blow the rock in question into bits about right for railroad ballast.

When he flashed the light on, the dust was still settling, and the Indians that had been crouched behind the missing rock had been reduced to what glistened like raspberry preserves spattered some distance down the slope. Seth had to flash twice more before they decided there'd been at least three of them by counting the larger lumps.

They'd just agreed on that when Little Dipper joined them to say both old Elmo and that greaser, Gordo, were going loco down below. Kid Wagner told the Texan, "Slide back down, and tell 'em we just killed, what, six of the rascals, Seth?"

"I make it seven, mayhaps eight, and I somehow doubt they'll try again up here this side of moonrise."

He squinted at the eastern horizon one could just make out now, and added, "The moon'll be coming up in no more than an hour now. Once it does that blackness along the base of the cliffs will look even blacker, so if I was leading 'em instead of trying to hold 'em off . . ."

"Gordo's got cur dogs staked out north and south in case Apache come pussyfooting in from either direction," Little Dipper cut in.

Seth nodded approvingly, and said, "It's good to hear I'm not stuck with all the thinking chores on our side. How's about sliding back on down and telling 'em we can likely hold this approach for now?"

Little Dipper said he'd do it. So Seth added, "Oh yeah, tell 'em I strung light bulbs over the rimrocks north and south, so I'll just flash 'em as need be, if I hear a dog barking serious down yonder."

Little Dipper laughed and left. It was Felicidad who asked Seth how he'd know which boulder below to blast if he couldn't see it, even with his ingenious wiring for sight and sound.

He sighed, and said, "I'm still working on that. I can't be everyplace at once. But let's hope the Apache don't have that figured yet."

The moon took its own sweet time. But nothing else had happened by the time it peeked over the ridges to their east like a lopsided pumpkin. Felicidad sighted her Mannlicher experimentally and opined she could hit anything bigger than a pack rat coming at them across the tilted expanse of bare, moonlit rock. Kid Wagner, smoking with his head below the flat top of their own boulder lest someone on the other side have as fine a rifle, decided, "They won't be back. They say Naiche and Geronimo only have a dozen or so followers apiece, and my daddy fit Indians under good old Colonel Chivington, riding with the Colorado Third Volunteers.''

Seth asked what that might have to do with here and now. Kid Wagner explained, ''My daddy said even white troops get mighty discouraged and hard to move forward once they've been whittled down a third. Indians discourage sooner, having less respect for their leaders pounded into 'em. So seeing we've just wiped out at least half the fighting force either Naiche or Geronimo could have had to start with . . .''

''We could be dealing with both bands,'' Seth cut in bleakly, only to add in a still more cheersome tone, ''Or another band entire of any size you'd like to guess at. Tom Horn told me some Apache scouts the army thought it had working for our side turned on old Al Sieber and lit out laughing, with lord knows how many army rifles or how much ammo.''

Kid Wagner nervously insisted Seth's surprisingly deadly ambushes had surely scared the fool Apache skinny. Felicidad sounded even less sure but said she was much more worried about her poor old father's fever than Apache obviously bent on suicide. Seth told her to ask Gordo for more eyes up in the rimrocks, seeing old Elmo didn't seem to care. She pointed out that as La Patrona she could detail as many of her own workers as she cared to and added that she'd make sure at least a couple of them spoke English.

She left her fancy rifle for Kid Wagner's use, should he need to use it. As she crawled away and rolled over the edge to work her way back down, Kid Wagner smiled wistfully after her, and murmured, ''Now there goes what I call a fine little lady, for a greaser. Do you have first dibs on her, Seth, or can any number play?''

Seth snorted in disbelief, and snapped, ''Hang some

crepe on your nose. Your brain lies dead inside your thick skull. Here we all are, fixing to get run over by Indians, and you're worried about my love life. Don't you cowboys ever think of anything else?''

The high plains rider took a deep reflective drag on his smoke, let it out, and decided, "Nope. Ain't none of us fixing to get out of this otherwise dull world alive and, in the end, all we'll have to show for our trouble is how many all-too-few good times we had betwixt too young and too old for some ring-dang-do.''

Seth told Wagner not to talk dirty with their mortal souls in such danger. The laconic cowhand inhaled smoke more soberly and let it out with a thoughtful sigh, saying, "You might be the one as ain't acting natural. My daddy said back when he was soldiering even the white gals seemed anxious to please. And everyone knows Indians go to war even more than we do because no Indian gal can let her boyfriend ride out of camp all smeared with paint afore she's encouraged him considerable with neither wearing nothing at all.''

Seth wrinkled his nose and said that sounded so romantic it made him want to puke. Kid Wagner insisted he'd settle for an Apache gal right now, provided she was a friendly one, of course, and added, "Leaving the obvious advantages aside, you could do yourself a heap worst than Miss Felicidad. Betwixt you and me, I suspicion that's one of the reasons old Elmo was fretting about the two of you spending so much time alone up here.''

Seth groaned, "Aw, for Pete's sake, you can see for yourself we were only blowing up Indians. Did Elmo say anything downright dirty about me and Miss Felicidad, damn it?''

Kid Wagner soothed, "Don't get your bowels in an uproar, old son. Nobody said you was playing slap-and-tickle on a rock with her sweet little enchilada. I suspicion

Elmo would find that a heap less vexing than he might more honorable intentions on your part.''

Seth laughed incredulously, and said, ''Madre de Díos, as I just learned to cuss from my intended! First you got me getting fresh with a highborn lady during an Indian attack, and now you're trying to get us engaged or worse?''

Kid Wagner chuckled, and said, ''I'll allow old Elmo seems to take the notion more serious than me. I like even darker greaser gals as, ah, dancing partners. But my poor old Calvinist mama would turn over in her grave if I brung home a bride of the papist persuasion.''

''Watch it,'' Seth warned flatly, adding, ''My mother's people were Dutch Reform, whilst my Canadian dad was from a Jacobite clan and sprinkled accordingly, Roman Catholic.''

Wagner assured him he wasn't looking for a religious argument, and added soothingly, ''So much the better for you if Miss Felicidad takes a real liking to you. Being a neither-nor, you'd get in no more trouble with the Lord than you're in already, and seeing she's pretty as well as rich . . .''

The penny dropped. Seth said, ''Elmo must be loco en la cabeza, which I think means out of his fool head. Does he really think I'd marry a gal for her gold mine?''

Kid Wagner shrugged, and said, ''I'll bet you either Elmo or that greaser, Gordo, would wed her at the friendly flutter of her eyelash. Her old man, Don Hernan, is sick as hell, and she's his only child. Gordo holds the Robles family has a proper mining claim as citizens by some sort of treaty. Elmo holds they're full of it unless he was blind the last time he looked up a never-recorded and long-abandoned claim. But either way, a gent married up with that pretty redhead would be in fair shape to take on all comers in court.''

Seth stood up and stretched, feeling safe to do as the

ever-rising moon cast her bright rays on everything within rifle range and then some. Somewhere in the night a dog was barking, not too friendly. Seth hunkered down to scoop up his tangle of wires and the battery box, saying, "Speaking of all comers, keep your eyes and that Mannlicher aimed down the slope for us whilst I see if I can find out what that pup's so riled about."

Suiting actions to his words, Seth walked partway to the edge and then dropped to crawl carefully the rest of the way when he felt some of the wires leading back downslope tighten up on him a mite.

Peering over the edge into the total blackness below, he made the proper contact and fed a plunger's worth of juice to the bulb dangling over the edge to the north of the mining site. He was getting used to the way the bulbs flashed when powered that way. The carbon filaments glowed from dull orange to bright white and then back to dull orange again at the bottom of the stroke. By moving the plunger just a tad slower, he could stretch out a somewhat duller light over a full second. When he did, his pals below spied a white-striped face glaring over a big rock at the tied-up yellow dog, too, and dusted said boulder with bullets fired long after the light had winked back out.

Seth doubted they'd hit anything. He had to study some on which lead he wanted this time, and his fingers were getting sort of tender from the sharp wires as well as the not-so-mild shocks. So he could only hope he had the right lead to the right rock when he set off the charge. Seth knew he had as soon as he flashed less lethal light down the craggy slope. For by the dull orange glow yet another figure in bloody white rags lay spread-eagled some ways north from where he'd been teasing the poor dog.

That appeared to have done it for now for the other side. From time to time Seth flashed the dangling light to the south as well, and he naturally asked Kid Wagner for advice on anything coming up the back slope toward them. But nothing happened until a quartet of Mexicans joined them topside, the one who spoke English, sort of, answering to the handle of Jose. He told them La Patrona was muy triste she'd forgotten her promise for to send them until the big bang down below had reminded her. Seth said he understood as soon as Jose added that her father, Don Hernan, was in mighty poor shape, even for an old man with the ague. When Seth asked how it looked to Jose the young Mex made the sign of the cross, and murmured, "Quíen sabe? When one considers the amount of oro this valle del muerto has ever yielded to the Robles family, it has cost them far too much. First the older brother, butchered by Loco's Apaches, and now Don Hernan, fading fast and not in much more comfort!"

Then he added pensively, "Perhaps if we bury him down in the mine shaft when it is over, Los Indios will not dig him up for to have fun with his manhood, eh?"

Seth grimaced, and replied, "You've no idea how much it cheers me to consider Indians castrating me even after they're done killing me!"

Jose said he wasn't looking forward to it either. Kid Wagner said his Indian-fighting dad thought Indians messed up dead folk to weaken their haunts, explaining, "Indians don't know they're all bound for hell and damnation when they die. They think that after you lay dead a spell you just wake up, sort of watered down and hard to see, of course, and go on about your usual business, which of course is devilment if you're an Indian. They ain't as smart as us about the reasons folk get sick. They suspect the haunts of dead enemies every time they catch cold or have a toothache. So they like to leave anyone they kill in piss-poor shape to haunt 'em, see?"

Seth dryly stated he felt sure he'd leave any Indian who killed him alone, no matter what. Jose said the few survivors of the last attack down below had been mighty sorry they'd buried their dead kith and kin so shallow, once they'd come up out of the mine shaft to find them so scattered about.

Seth tried to picture poor old Benny carrying on like that, the old gent being so polite to talk to. Of course, when he'd finally had enough guff off Hamp Ferris, he hadn't been so polite about it. He wondered if the pals of those Chiricahua he'd just made good Indians out of pictured him as some sort of grinning fiend. He figured they likely did. The question before the house was what they aimed to do about it. What Kid Wagner's dad had said about the casualties a fighting outfit could accept before they decided they'd had all the fighting they wanted for now made a heap of sense. On the other hand the army had skunked Geronimo over and over, and, say what one would about him being a liar and a cheat, nobody could deny he was one fighting son of a bitch.

But whether they were still lurking out there in the dark or not, it appeared they'd pulled back to reconsider their options by the time the moon had risen high enough to bathe the bases of the cliffs in the same ghostly glow it was shedding on the rimrocks and rooftops a mite closer to the sparkling water running down the once-more peaceful-looking valley.

Seth smoked down a cigar of his own, fighting back the urge to yawn. Then he moved back to the rock Kid Wagner still sat up against, removed his own hat for a pillow, and said, "I'm going to see if I can catch a wink or more. Wake me up if we get attacked by Apache."

Kid Wagner said he would. Jose told them both not to worry about that, assuring them such attacks seldom lasted long enough for anyone to wake up all the way.

But the next time Seth opened his eyes the sun was shining, and when he sat up to stare about, the world looked bright and innocent as ever, save where a few shattered corpses lay on the sunlit rock. So Seth went down to see what they might be serving for breakfast.

They were doling out beans and rice. The mujer who filled his bowl was the one who told him Don Hernan had woke up dead that morning.

Seth had been hungry up until then. He settled for half a tin cup of coffee, swallowed, and swished his mouth fresh with the rest before heading for the Robles cabin to pay his respects. Before he could round the corner of the main building, Elmo Dawson cut him off, saying, "You done us proud last night, old son. Now we got more serious things to worry about."

Seth smiled uncertainly and asked what in thunder could be more serious than an Indian attack. Elmo said, "Old man Robles just died on us. Whether he had any lawsome claim on this mine or not, he can't have it now. We don't want either his daughter or that uglier Gordo jumping a dead man's claim ahead of us. So we're going to have to study on what's to be done about both of 'em."

Seth stared incredulously at the older man, shook his head, and decided, "You must be trying to prove what they say about gold having the power to drive some roothogs goofy! We're cut off from any fool claims court by Lord knows how many unreconstructed Apache, Elmo! Do you really think this would be the smart time to start fighting among ourselves?"

The other gringo's eyes glittered with greed as he answered, simply, "There'll never be a better time to get the drop on 'em. Gordo and his boys have us badly outnumbered, boy. Do we give that fat greaser time to get set up first. . . ."

"He'll prove he's as big a pig and as silly a sap as you are!" Seth cut in, adding, "Whether he is or he ain't, the other Mexicans call Miss Felicidad their Patrona, which means about what it sounds like. So they won't do anything serious for Gordo without asking her about it first.''

Elmo's thin smile got downright dangerous as he quietly replied, ''I don't much cotton to being called a pig or a sap, boy.''

Seth shrugged and asked, ''Does Apache suit you better? I'll allow you looks as pale of face as the rest of us, but white men worth spit stand by the Good Book and the U.S. Constitution, and there's nothing in neither saying you got a right to grab a gold mine just because you want it and figure you're tough enough to take it.''

Elmo tried, ''Be reasonsome, boy. These greasers never filed no proper claim and, damn it, you signed on to work for *me*, not *them*!''

Seth replied soberly, ''Let's not debate apples and oranges as have nothing to do with one another. Miss Felicidad says her family's owned this mine from way back when under U.S. as well as Mex mining laws.''

''She's full of it. I tell you I made a title search and proved to my own satisfaction that the gold was up for grabs!'' Elmo insisted.

Seth said, ''Be that as it may, white men settle such disputes in court, and it's Apache as just takes what they want by brute force with a clear conscience. You hired me to protect you from such ruthless gents and, leaving aside the part about seeing some of your money, up to now, I never signed on as your pet Apache raider, and that's what you're asking of me, you know. White outlaws such as Frank and Jesse James have been known to leave their victims living in the end. What you just proposed is pure massacre a decent Indian would think twice about, there being women and children in this camp as well as Gordo and his boys.''

Dawson scowled, and snapped, "Hold on, I never said nothing about hurting no women and children."

But Seth insisted, "That's funny, you don't look that dumb. Are you trying to tell me even you could grab a going gold mine, leaving witnesses to your grab alive and free to take you to law on civil as well as criminal charges?"

Neither man had deliberately raised his voice in all this time. But the daggers they'd been shooting with their eyes, or perhaps the serious way each had planted his own boots and gun hand, had been noticed at some distance. So as Kid Wagner and Virgin Joe drifted in to see if anyone wanted to tell them what was up, Elmo Dawson pasted a friendlier smile than he could have felt across his sweaty face, and said, "We'll talk about it later, old son. Meanwhile, if you want to keep that pretty Mex gal buttered up and on our side, don't let me stop you."

Seth hesitated. Then, not wanting to push it any further than he had to, he nodded curtly and moved on. As he rounded the corner of the main log outbuilding he became aware of Kid Wagner striding in step on his left. When Wagner asked what that had been about back there, Seth told him to ask Dawson if he just couldn't stand to mind his own beeswax.

The high plains rider answered simply, "It *is* my beeswax when I see a man who owes me a heap of back pay about to slap leather. I hope you settled the matter with him or, failing that, I hope you have a good reason. Some of the others are already wondering how he's ever going to pay us off as he promised, seeing the greasers never gave up this gold mine after all."

Seth took a deep breath, let half of it out so his voice would sound calm, and replied, "He wanted the seven of us to gun down all the Mexicans so's any of us left could have them Apache all to ourselves. I think I talked him out of it for now.''

Kid Wagner gave a long, low whistle. Seth said, ''See-ing you wanted to talk beeswax, where might you stand if old Elmo and I had to settle the matter for good, man to man?''

Kid Wagner never hesitated as he said, ''As far out of the line of fire as I could manage. No offense, but I don't like either of you boys enough to risk my own sweet ass and, seeing you're both sort of handy with guns . . .''

''What about the others?'' Seth cut in; and this time Wagner had to ponder some before he decided, ''I can't see either of the dippers mixing into a private fight unin-vited. Like you and me, those two met Elmo recent and haven't seen the color of his money yet.''

Seth asked, ''What about Pinto and Virgin Joe?''

Wagner shrugged, and said, ''Can't say for sure. Pinto was cooking for old Elmo the first night I camped with 'em back near Deming. Old Virgin Joe joined up ahead of me and the dippers as well. Being from the Nevada mining country, he'd know better than you or me whether Elmo's plan makes any sense or not. It sounds a mite raw to this old cow thief, too. But he was telling us one night how claim jumpers took the Comstock Lode at Virginia City away from the poor old gent as struck the first color and, looking back on it, Virgin Joe seemed to feel they'd been slickers he'd always envied a heap.''

They strode on a ways before Wagner decided, ''If ever I found my fool self in your boots, I'd worry most about Elmo, then Pinto and Virgin Joe, in that order. You should have took him back there, just now, when you had the chance.''

Seth dryly asked what Wagner had been drinking. The older and more experienced saddle tramp replied as dryly, ''I took the pledge for now when I saw the greasers poison that Apache yesterday. You might say I'm cautious by nature. That's how come I try not to cross a man with Elmo Dawson's rep to begin with, and why, when I *do* have to, I prefers to get it over with, one way or the other, and not have to worry about a bullet in the back from then on.''

"I doubt old Elmo could be that sore at me," Seth protested.

Wagner asked, "Why couldn't he? You just backed him down, didn't you? I wouldn't be here now if Virgin Joe hadn't spied what was going on from afar and said it looked like a showdown for sure.''

Seth cast an uneasy glance back the way they'd just come, seeing nobody more important than a couple of kids fooling around as he decided, "Old Joe's no doubt having much the same sort of conversation with old Elmo right now. I'm trying to decide whether you're a born troublemaker, too. I sure wish a man got to pick his own fights in these parts.''

Kid Wagner chuckled fondly and told him he was free to fight all the gents he felt like fighting, as long as he didn't want anyone to pitch in. Then he asked where they were going.

Seth pointed at the private quarters of the late Don Hernan and his sole survivor just up the slope, saying, "Thought I'd pay my respects and ask when they meant to bury the old geezer. If there's anything me and folk of the Hebrew persuasion agree on it's short wakes and planting 'em sudden, even when it's cooler and there ain't wild Indians in the neighborhood.''

Kid Wagner said he'd never gotten to watch a Jewish burial.

Seth said he didn't make a habit of it, but explained, "This shopkeeper down the Third River at Davis Crossing had always traded with us fair. So we had to go when he fell dead from a heart stroke one morning. I asked this

Jewish boy I got to talking with how come they seemed
to be burying the old gent in such unseemly haste. He said
their custom was to get their dead below ground before
the sun went down. Makes a heap of sense as soon as you
study on it. Friends and relations feel bad enough without
having to watch you turning funny colors in the front par-
lor. There was this one family over by Dodd's Mill, kept
a fat old lady on view close to a week in the dog days of
August and, man . . ."

Kid Wagner said he felt no call to view dead Mexicans,
even fresh ones, and peeled off to go bother someone else.
As Seth approached the front steps of the Robles cabin, he
saw six or eight men and women of the old gent's persuasion lined up outside the open doorway. So he doffed his
own hat, too, and got in line behind a nice-looking Mex
gal with a baby wrapped in a shawl and braced on one of
her hips. She seemed surprised to see him there and offered to let him in line ahead of her, if he was guessing
right at her soft, shy Spanish. He finally managed to convince her, in English, things were just fine.

After he'd stood there a time, the young Mex called Jose
came out on the veranda to tell him they wanted him inside. When Seth asked what about these others ahead of
him, Jose insisted La Patrona wanted him right now, and
that it was important. So Seth told the Mexicans ahead of
him he was sorry, and from the way they smiled back at
him, he figured they likely followed his drift.

Inside, with the window drapes all drawn, Don Hernan
lay atop the bedding in a black-and-silver trimmed charro
outfit that made him look a heap less old and sick. He still
looked mighty dead, with a silk kerchief slung under his
pale jaws and knotted atop his gray head to keep his mouth
shut and silver coins doing much the same for his eyelids.
Felicidad, all in black, had been seated on a baby-blue

straight-back chair near the head of the bed until she saw Seth coming in and rose to greet him. He took the hand she held out to him and, not knowing the exact form, just hung on to it, saying, "The other boys asked me to express their own sorrow about all this, ma'am."

She raised one eyebrow dubiously, and told him softly, "All walls have ears, and walls of logs are even easier to hear through. Jose just told me about your conversation with Señor Dawson. I'm afraid that as soon as Gordo hears about it . . ."

"Let's make sure he doesn't hear about it then," Seth cut in, adding, "I've already dealt Wagner and those two young Texas cow hands out of the game."

She insisted, "That still leaves it three against one if Señor Dawson is really serious."

He nodded, but said, "I doubt he's as serious as Gordo would likely get if we didn't let sleeping dogs lie. I don't want to brag, but all three of those boys know I carry five in the wheel and shoot pretty straight. If Jose was listening in, he should have told you Elmo had his chance to show his stuff, fair and square, only he never, and Virgin Joe at least should be smart enough to see that, no matter how he might feel about claim jumping."

She repressed a shudder, and murmured, "I fail to see what my people have ever done to deserve both Los Apaches and Los Americanos at once in this small corner of the world. I mean no disrespect and I know last night you probably saved a good many if not all our lives, pero es verdad the situation was much easier to understand before the seven of you rode in!"

He smiled thinly, and soothed, "It could have been worse; in the beginning there was nine of us and one was Apache, or Na Déné as he chose to call his somewhat surly self."

Young Jose had been standing by the doorway up to

now. When he cleared his throat and came over to join them, muttering something about the time, Felicidad nodded and told Seth she had to get back to receiving respects before it got too hot to stand in line outside. So Seth said he had plenty of chores to tend as well, and she told Jose to tag after him and back his play in Spanish in case anyone decided to do something stupid.

Once outside Jose asked where they might be headed next, to do what. Seth said, ''Supply shed for openers. I don't know what those power surges from the battery box do to Edison bulbs. I know they're made for around forty watts at about a hundred volts of direct and steady current. That's how come they flash a mite brighter when you really put your back into the short, quick charge meant to detonate dynamite caps. That can't be good for 'em, and I'd surely hate to have to worry about blown-out bulbs in the middle of an Indian attack come sundown. So I mean to just replace the old ones whilst the replacing's good. May as well connect more dynamite charges to all them wires we used up last night, too. You only lose a yard or so of the far end when you shoot the juice on down such wires.''

Jose said, ''I saw that when we scraped up the Indio you shredded for us just to the north last night. Pero Gordo says, and I agree, it seems unlikely they will try to move in on us that way again, if they are still out there at all, after losing so many muchachos.''

Seth shrugged, said it was always better to feel safe than sorry, and stepped out into the full sunlight to head on over to the sandbagged explosives shed. Since Jose still seemed to be with him, Seth asked what they'd done with the dead Apache. Jose said they'd buried them as well as the one Gordo had poisoned in the mine tailings. When Seth found this confusing even in English, Jose explained, ''For every ounce of gold more than a ton of crushed quartz is left over, ground muy fine, like flour for to bake tortillas, for to get all the gold out, so . . .''

"I noticed them big dirt piles as we arrived," Seth cut in. When he asked about the bodies on the far side of the rimrocks above them Jose shrugged.

"Los buitres have to live, too, eh?"

Seth started to ask a dumb question but decided, "Buitres must be what we call buzzards, right?"

Jose grinned, and said, "Sí, safer for the muchachos we got looking out up there if they stay behind that one big rock near the edge. Plenty buitres up there, and it makes Los Indios watching from the chaparral further down muy muy melancolico. They think it bad for an hombre's espiritu when his cadaver is torn apart. That is for why they tear us up after they kill us. I bet they think you kill good as they can, eh?''

Seth modestly allowed he'd been raised to do the job right or not do it at all. As they entered the explosives shed Jose glanced back outside as if to make sure they were having a private conversation before he suddenly blurted, out of context, "La Patrona told me to say nothing to the others about your fight with the one called Elmo, pero just the same . . .''

"Hold on, it was only a disagreement, not a fight," Seth cut in.

Jose shrugged, and said, "I heard what I heard. That you are not a gringo perfido is not the question. The question is which one of you Americanos is in command? We know the one called Elmo says he is your Patron. Pero up until now he has done nothing but cast envious eyes on both our patrona and her family holdings.''

Seth started to say something, but Jose insisted, "It has been remarked that you are the only one, save perhaps for your cook, who seems to know what he is doing here. It was you who blew up all those Indios. It was you the other

Americanos took orders from last night, while the one called Elmo was hiding somewhere in the dark.''

Seth looked uncomfortable as he pried open the top of a pine box of fresh dynamite sticks cradled in sawdust. He ran an experimental finger along one as he muttered, ''This stuff should be stored in a cooler place, but, thank God, the sawdust's soaked up any nitro that's beaded out so far. I don't see the strychnine Gordo spiked that firewater with around here, do you?''

Jose said Gordo used nux vomica, and that they kept it in the main building to deal with rats, even if the label on the gallon cans did say it was for coyotes.

Seth replied, ''Nux vomica's the mighty sinister tree seeds they start out with. Strychnine's the purified poison, and from the way that Chiricahua contorted, he'd just taken his poison pretty near to neat.''

Jose cheerfully agreed rats damned near tied themselves in knots after just a taste of the stuff. The boy asked hopefully whether Seth wanted some for the useless Elmo Dawson.

Seth shot the Mex a stern look, and warned, ''Never play with the notion of killing anyone you ain't serious about killing. It's a good way to wind up dead your ownself. What you just said is a living example of what I mean. You overheard old Elmo only toying with the notion of jumping Miss Felicidad's claim, and now you're toying with his death and destruction as well!''

Jose shrugged, and said, ''I don't think he was only toying with the idea. I know I'm not.''

Seth replied he hadn't heard that and explained there might be other uses for strychnine than killing rats. Then he put more dynamite, caps to go with it, and some extra light bulbs in an empty box, saying, ''They say the devil finds work for idle hands, and talking idle can get you in a heap of trouble, too. So let's get back to work.''

Jose tried, but well before high noon he got tired of following Seth all over and watching him do mysterious gringo chores. So Seth found himself alone by the time he'd replaced the last Edison bulb and lowered the socket back down the cliff on its wire. The clear glass bulb he'd just removed looked sound enough, albeit a mite blackened near the nipple where they sucked all the air out back in his own home state. So the apparently still-intact filament had likely suffered some from flashing so brightly, however briefly. Rejoining the two Mexican kids by the big rock he'd shared with Felicidad under spookier lighting conditions, he held up the bulb, and told them, ''They make these things less'n a day's ride from our dairy barn back home. You want to see something neat?''

Neither spoke English, so they just giggled nervously. They laughed more natural when he lofted the bulb as high as he could get it to go underhanded and got it to bang like a firecracker when it finally came down to implode on the solid rock.

This inspired the buzzards huddled here and there on the slope to scatter skyward. Once he got a better look at what the birds had been huddled over, Seth was inspired to slide back down the cleft to camp, leaving the amused Mex kids to hold his nighttime command post until such time as he might be called upon to take over up there again.

He saw they were serving tortillas and beans on the rear veranda of the main hall now. Recalling he'd missed breakfast with a sudden pang, he ambled over to get in line. Once he'd done so he felt hungry as a bitch wolf and groped absently for a smoke before he remembered he was out of 'em. The Texan they called Little Dipper used that as an excuse to bust into line with him, saying, ''Have a seegar, Jersey Lilly. Where've you been all this time?

Me and the boys was just jawing about you, and Pinto gave this to me, knowing I don't smoke.''

Seth struck a match to light the cheroot he'd been given before he replied he'd just been here, there, and everywhere a fool Indian might choose to wind up after dark, adding, ''Lord willing they're long gone. We gave 'em a good dusting last night, and Geronimo seems to surrender every time the army draws any blood at all.''

Little Dipper said, ''We ain't the army, and it ain't likely we're dealing with either of them bands off the San Carlos Agency.''

He saw he had Seth's interest and continued, ''I've been trying to make friends, speaking some Spanish and seeing some of the gals here ain't downright deformed. This one Yaqui gal, Ynez, says neither the one you blowed up at the base of the cliffs nor the one who hogged all the coyote bait they gave him for his chief was dressed in the right kind of cotton.''

Seth asked him to back up and explain both Yaqui gals and the kind of cotton they might be jawing about. So Little Dipper said, ''Yaqui are Mex Indians about as tough as Apache only different and, lucky for us, they don't like Apache at all.''

Seth said, ''Nobody seems to. What was that about cotton again?''

The Texan explained. ''Ynez says our Indian agents issue machine-wove white muslin to our own Indians as might need any. El Presidente Diaz down Mexico way holds that nobody has the right to act all that Indian this long after Cortez told 'em all to put on some decent pants and show up for next Sunday's Mass if they aimed to go on living.''

Seth took a step nearer the three gals dealing out the grub and told Little Dipper to get to the damned point.

The Texan said, ''Neither Yaqui nor any other Mex Indians pay any more attention to their officious government than our redskins mind old Grover Cleveland. But the point is that no matter how they dress south of the border, they don't get to use U.S. issue muslin. Ynez says the cotton both them Apache had on was hand-wove on strap looms, making them Mex-bred Nedli or at best Mescalero and certainly not Chiricahua, see?''

Seth didn't answer as the fat gals handed him a bowl of beans, a couple of tortillas, and a cup of coffee in turn. As he watched them grub Little Dipper up, he said, "I liked it better the other way. What would Mex-bred Apache be doing up this way when it's Chiricahua, and only two bands at that, on the warpath right now, damn their muly hides?''

As the two of them moved down the veranda with their grub, Little Dipper replied, "You just said yourself, they had muly hides. But according to Ynez the Mexican Federales, that's their army, likely see a good chance to settle their own Apache problem, as long as it's so noisy this summer in any case.''

By tacit agreement they sat down on some steps in the shade to set their coffee aside and dig into the beans with rolled-up tortillas as Little Dipper continued. "Mexico don't mess around with willsome Indians. That's likely why they've never had half the trouble with 'em. Instead of waiting for Apache and such to act up, Los Federales just go after 'em, with or without no excuse, whenever they figure they have the chance to box 'em.''

Seth washed down a wad of tortillas and beans, then nodded and said, "Miss Felicidad said something before about Mexican troops being out and trigger-happy. Knowing our own Apache scare has our army out in force with field artillery, the Mexicans are out to play nutcracker with Apache in general, right?''

Little Dipper nodded, and said, "Ynez is scared they'll

turn on her Yaqui kin as soon as they get done with Indios they hate even worse. I told her not to worry, because nobody's harder to wipe out than Apache. Pound for pound the wiry little sons of bitches are tougher to get rid of than skeeters in a swamp.''

Seth went on eating a spell before he reflected, ''We might have swatted enough around here to afford us a breather. But I sure wish you hadn't told me about 'em likely being on the run from an even meaner army than our own. Am I right in assuming Mexico doesn't give an Indian a second chance once he violates the terms of his first surrender?''

Little Dipper laughed, and said, ''Hell, neither does Texas. How did you think we calmed down our Comanche? The damn yankee notion you can trust a man who's word's no good as long as he's a sulky savage is as dumb as saying train robbers don't have to go to prison as long as they'll just get off the train and accept another hand-out.''

He washed down some of his beans and added petulantly, ''Of course, it don't cut no ice to say you're sorry if you're a white boy facing trial for murder, rape, or, hell, shoplifting. That's how come we get to behave ourselves, and Indians don't have to. Mexico has the right idea. You tell the silly son of a bitch to pay his bills and obey the law like everyone else, and if he don't you kill him same as any other outlaw.''

Seth said, ''Let's not worry about Mexico's Indian policy. Right now I'm more worried about their Indians. I can see why they want this valley. Hell, I can see why they *need* this valley. They need the water, wood, and grazing at least as much as we need any gold mine, and . . .''

''That's what the boys wanted me to ask you about,'' the Texan cut in, casting a cautious eye about to see if anyone else had an ear cocked his way as he continued. "The boys all heard about the same story from old Elmo back in Deming. The plan was to back his play for this gold claim on the sort of vague understanding we'd all wind up prosperous in the sweet by-and-by."

Seth said cautiously, "I'm sure he really thought the Robles family had been wiped out by the last Apache attack. He'd have never laid out good money on ponies, guns, supplies, and such if he'd thought he was leading us all on a wild goose chase."

Little Dipper put his cup and bowl aside, belched, and reached for fresh snuff as he softly gowled, "Mebbe. I can't help noticing none of us have seen dime one of that dollar a day he promised back in town. Try her this way. Say he knew from the start the greasers had never given up this claim. Say he figured once we'd gone to all this trouble to find it with him, miles from the nearest law in times of considerable confusion, we'd likely find all these greasers in the way of fame and fortune, if you follow my drift."

Seth nodded soberly, and said, "I already told him I don't commit murder for no dollar a day. How do you and the boys feel about that?"

Little Dipper spat thoughtfully, and said, "Pinto says hired guns draw at least five hundred a month just glaring. Costs a boss more if he expects them to fight serious for him."

Seth didn't answer, figuring the Texan would get to the point in his own good time. Then Little Dipper told Seth, "We figured, you having the Indian sign on old Elmo, we'd let you decide what's fair and how we ought to go about getting it. None of us are all that greedy, you understand, but it do stand to reason that after all the trouble we've gone to we ought to come out some pocket-jingle ahead."

Seth stared at him incredulously, and replied, "How do you feel about winding up no worse than you started, alive and well, back in Deming, which could be one hell of an improvement over where we all are at the moment?"

Little Dipper spat uncertainly, and asked, "You mean without no money at all to show for all this shit?"

Seth nodded soberly, and insisted, "It's not as if we've all been blowing our own money on whisky and wanton women along the way, you know. It's almost the Fourth of July, and they'll be signing extra hands on for the fall roundup before you know it."

Little Dipper looked away, and asked softly, "What about this gold mine we come all this way to find?"

So there it was, out in the open, like a gob of his brown spit; and all Seth could reply was, "What about it? Do you really think the six of you could lick all these Mexicans and then lick all those Apache, too?"

Little Dipper softly protested, "I make it *seven* on our side, Jersey Lilly."

Seth shook his head and said, "Suicide ain't my style. Even if it was, we just agreed a dollar a day seems piss-poor pay for such heavy work."

Little Dipper looked uncomfortable as he replied, "We had something more like even shares in the claim in mind. If you don't want in, can we count on you just sitting out the dance at least?"

Seth gathered his empty cup and bowl to rise to his feet again as he decided. "Depends on the music and the step. Ignoring the screams of women and children ain't my style neither."

He headed back to the fat gals with his cup and bowl. When he saw Little Dipper was still with him, he added, "The Third River, back home, ain't much as a rule. But once or more every summer it overflows its banks and runs mean and muddy, drowning kids, cows, and other dumb critters.''

"What's that got to do with things out here?" asked Little Dipper, glancing anxiously at the clear cobalt sky above them. "Are you saying we got flash floods to worry about, too?"

Seth handed his used cup and bowl to one of the Mex women with a nod of thanks and a try at "Gracias." When she demurely said, "Por nada!" Seth turned back to the Texan to explain, "Wasn't talking about out there. I was recalling the time I jumped into the Third River, in full flood, to save the mean old Widow Van Tassel. Lord knows how the ugly old fuss ever wound up bobbing down the current with all her duds on, screaming fit to bust, but there she was, and there I went, and the next thing I knew we were on our way to Oates Mills with the loony old thing hitting me over the head with her walking stick and accusing me of trying to feel her up underwater.''

Little Dipper laughed at the picture and asked how they'd ever made out. Seth soberly stated, "We both drowned, of course. The hell of it was she never even thanked any of us after we got her dried out and back to her own. But to tell the truth, if we did have us a flash flood here, and the Widow Van Tassel went screaming by us with her cane, I'd likely feel obliged to leap in and haul her out some more.''

By now they were back on the gravel slope of the mining camp with a clear view of the little creek in question. Little Dipper stared dubiously at the bare trickle, and said, "I follow your drift, and that redheaded Robles gal ain't no ugly old widow woman. I don't imagine you've asked her how a good man with a gun might come out working for her side, huh?"

Seth shook his head, but said, "I can see what you might imagine, and I can see how far I'd get with you and the boys if I thought it important to convince you otherwise. So let's just say I mean to do what I have to do when the time comes to do it. Satisfied?''

Little Dipper shrugged, and said, ''Like the old song says, farther along we'll know more about it. Might not be a showdown at all if half the others are as easygoing as you about *gold*.''

Seth said he certainly hoped so. He knew better than to count on it. Gold sure could cause a heap of trouble when you considered the stuff by itself. Seth had read in a schoolbook about the argument Pizarro had had about gold with the Grand Inca, that time he'd conquered Peru. The Grand Inca, Atahualpa, hadn't been able to see why the Spaniards were so mad about gold, seeing they already had glass and iron the Indians found more astonishing. Pizarro had wanted gold more than he'd wanted an argument. So he told Atahualpa his own people had a loathsome disease that could only be cured by gold. Miss Bish, their history teacher, had allowed that in each one's way they'd both been right. Seth had only recently understood exactly what the wise old gal must have meant.

It wasn't as a metal, less useful than brass the same color, that ounces of gold could cost tons of grief. It was the tons of nicer stuff that ounces of gold could buy. Old Benny had still thought of gold as yellow iron. Yet, knowing more about the cash economy of the outside world, he'd been ready as any white man to risk his red hide for a crack at the stuff.

Thinking of Benny made Seth think about other Apache, foreign or domestic, who might or might not still be out there. He headed back to the Robles cabin to talk to Felicidad about that. On the way he was intercepted by her segundo, Gordo. The burly Mex seemed to have something on his own mind. Seth stopped, nodded, and said,

"I'm glad I run across you first. Might save me getting a lady's hopes up premature."

Gordo growled, "La Patrona is in mourning, gringo. Can you not wait until Don Hernan is in his coffin before you covet his daughter?"

Seth smiled thinly at the heftier Gordo, and said, "I sure admire a man with a vivid imagination. But before either of us comes courting with flowers, books, and candy, can we agree it might be best for all concerned if we got Miss Felicidad and all the other gals out of this grim spot?"

Gordo asked suspiciously, "Pero dónde, y cómo? We dare not make a run for Deming with Apache out there, anywhere, just waiting for us to try."

He looked even less friendly as he added suspiciously, "Of course, if Los Indios are no longer out there, all La Patrona could hope to gain from such a long ride would be the loss of her gold mine, eh?"

Seth swore softly, and said, "Miss Bish was right. Nobody can think halfway straight about yellow iron. Nobody can steal a gold mine, Gordo. Not if it's proper owner has the brains of a gnat. Miss Felicidad told me her kin have been U.S. citizens since the treaty of '48, and that their original Mexican claim was transferred and recorded as an American mine. Was she lying to me?"

Gordo shook his head, and growled, "No, pero gringo lawyers lie in gringo courts before gringo judges about the rights of La Raza. Doña Felicidad may be white of skin and red of hair, es verdad. Pero she is still a greaser, as well as a *woman*, in the eyes of any New Mexico court."

"Come on," Seth insisted. "Women may not have the vote or the right to go to war with other U.S. citizens, but it ain't as if they ain't allowed to own property, Gordo. I was just now talking about an old widow woman as held a hundred and sixty acres of prime bottom land in her own name, once she'd buried old Caleb Van Tassel.''

Gordo insisted, ''She was not a Robles fighting for her rights in New Mexico Territory. If she was a man, or married to a man with hair on his chest . . . Pero don't you even *think* about it, muchacho!''

Seth snorted in disgust, and said, ''I haven't been, but don't push your luck with me. I was talking about getting Miss Felicidad and the rest of us out of here. You'd know better than me if you have enough riding stock in your remuda to make a break for it tonight.''

Gordo didn't hesitate. He shook his head firmly, and replied, ''La Patrona has already asked me that. I told her there was an outside chance she and a handful of body-guards might make it if the rest of us offered some sort of diversion for Los Indios. There are not enough ponies for everyone, even with the smaller children riding double with their parents. There is no way for to ride out without leaving at least ten or twelve behind. Do I have to tell you how La Patrona feels about that?''

Seth said, ''Not hardly. If there's one thing we agree on, Gordo, it has to be that Miss Felicidad's a real lady.''

They didn't exactly bury Don Hernan that afternoon. The mine had been worked long enough to afford more than one cul-de-sac. So Felicidad thought it best to en-tomb him in a dry one, and Seth was glad. For by half-past three it had really gotten hot above ground, and there was no way to embalm the poor old gent this far from civilization.

Seth tagged along respectfully but didn't follow Felici-dad and her funeral party down into the mine. So he was seated on a dynamite box just to one side of the adit when Elmo Dawson caught up with him. When Seth said Elmo could still catch the funeral, if that was his intention, the older would-be mine owner shook his head, and said, "It was you I wanted a word with. Little Dipper told me what you said about carrying honesty to the point of stupidity, and here I find you guarding that greaser gal's safe return from the bowels of this old earth. Are you worried about somebody caving in a gold mine with your redhead somewheres under the mountain, Jersey Lilly?"

Seth casually got to his feet as he replied. "I wish you'd try to make more sense. To begin with the lady ain't nobody's redhead as far as I know, and I doubt anybody here would want to try and cave in her mine, whether she was down in it or not."

Seth was aware Pinto and both the dippers were drifting up-slope to join them, leaving Kid Wagner and Virgin Joe as unknown factors so far. Dawson didn't have to turn his head to know they were there as he sort of purred, "How come? How many rounds might you be able to pack in the wheel of that Jesse James Schofield, old son?"

Seth spread his boot heels just a tad as the three backing Elmo stopped, expressionless, just inside easy pistol range, as if it was up to old Elmo to call the next tune. Seth knew it likely was as he answered easily, "We all know how many times a six-shooter shoots. But that ain't the question before the house. The question before the house is what in thunder would anyone want with a caved-in gold mine?"

He saw the two dippers exchanging not-too-bright but worried looks. He quickly added, "Even if you got to reopen it later with an Anglo crew of hardrockers, you'd surely have a time explaining all those dead Mexican folk they'd have to muck through to get back at the high-grade, right?"

Elmo shrugged, and said, "Dead folk tell no tales, old son."

Seth shook his head, and said, "I'd hate to bank my

neck on that. They hang you high in this territory for murdering even a Mexican in cold blood for gain, and how would anyone know for sure what anyone might or might not have to say, this side of digging them up again, I mean?''

Elmo growled, ''What are you talking about, boy? We're never in this world going to have that gal, her segundo, and half her fighting men in such a handy spot all at once. As to anyone accusing anyone of anything, after they've been dead a spell . . .''

''They call it literacy,'' Seth cut in, adding, ''Didn't you go to school at all, Elmo? I know Miss Felicidad can read and write. Some of the others might, even if it's only in Spanish. So how might anyone bury that many folk in a mine alive and not be worried about even one of 'em writing a word or more with, say, the black stub of a torch on rock if not with a handier pencil and paper.''

Little Dipper spat, murmured something to his fellow Texan, and turned away. Big Dipper stared after him a short time, shrugged, and followed. When Pinto called out to them neither turned to look back.

Pinto sighed, and said, ''I dunno, boss. Even if we can take him, I don't see how we'll have enough time to work with.''

Elmo sighed, and said, ''You talk too much, you blotch-faced boob! Did anybody here say word one about anybody taking anybody? Me and old Seth are still thick as thieves, ain't that right, amigo mio?''

Seth shrugged, and said, ''Well, I ain't sure how thick I want to be with thieves. On the other hand, as I keep trying to convince all the damned fools I keep meeting out here in Apacheria, this seems neither the time nor the place for civilized folk to fight one another.''

Elmo Dawson nodded almost too agreeably, and said, ''My feelings exactly. A man just doesn't have much use for pocket-jingle after Apache skin his ass, pants and all. I don't know where you got the notion I was planning to fight anyone but Chiricahua, old son."

Seth said, "If they were Chiricahua they're likely long gone. If they're from south of the border they're likely still around. Didn't Little Dipper tell you what that Indian gal on our side said about the ones we've killed so far?"

Elmo grimaced, and said, "Something about Mescalero. Who pays attention to even a white woman when the discussion concerns Indians?"

Seth said, "Me. What she said makes sense. If they're as desperate and far from home as she said, they'll surely be back for more after sundown. We got off easy last night, because they couldn't have been expecting half the tricks we pulled on 'em. But old soldiers never die because they don't stumble into the same trap all that often."

Pinto moved closer to stand beside Dawson as he snorted and opined, "There's no way they can get at us any other way, and we got plenty of dynamite left."

Seth answered dryly, "I'm sure you're right about that. Meanwhile I've already blasted away half the obvious cover a skirmisher would drop behind by instinct. I likely blasted away the Indians most prone to approach that way as well. By now they've had a whole day to reconsider the way they tried last night. If they try again, you can bet your hides, and you will be, that they won't come in at us the same way."

Dawson asked in sincere interest how Seth figured they might get hit the next time. Seth replied, "Do I look like an Apache general? If I was I'd likely try a spread-out skirmish line coming down that more open and gentle slope across the stream. I know it would be suicidal right now, in broad daylight with half of us firing high-powered rifles from good cover. But come nightfall I don't see how anyone's supposed to aim gun one at a redskin scooting crabways in the dark until he's right on top of you.''

Elmo grimaced, and said, ''That sounds like the makings of a mighty nasty state of total confusion, kid.''

Seth nodded, and said, ''I hear that's why they paint them broad white stripes across their sweet faces. It's just the kind of fighting they're so famous for and none of us are. If it's any consolation, both sides ought to take ferocious losses in that kind of a fight. The question is who can best afford to, along with who really has to. I asked Gordo before how he felt about trying for a bustout. He said we don't have enough stock to take everyone along without we overload at least some of the ponies, making 'em carry double.''

Pinto repressed a shudder, and declared flatly, ''If there is one thing this child will never do, at gunpoint, riding double in the dark with Apache chasing me has to be it!''

Dawson nodded soberly, and said, ''We're way better off forted up and letting the red devils come to us.''

Seth insisted, ''Depends on how many times how many of 'em come at us. They know how many of us there are and where to find us in the dark at their own bloodthirsty pleasure. If we're only talking a dozen or so you're not only right, but they'll know you're right and never even try. On the other hand we've barely the strength of an army platoon, even not fighting one another, and how many troopers was it that Custer had with him about this time of the year in '76?''

Elmo Dawson turned to stare west against the dazzle of the late afternoon sun, musing half to himself, ''Hmm, if we knew for sure, and you set up some more charges and them electicated lights before sundown . . .''

''I can't,'' Seth cut in, adding, ''Already studied on it, of course. My big surprise last night was that they weren't expecting either the planted charges or the flashing lights.

Tonight they will be, and there's just no way I can mine that slope and set up Edison bulbs without them marking every position from the distance and making sure nobody goes anywhere near either. But about those ponies . . . I suspect they've counted both human and pony heads from afar by now and likely agree with Gordo. So they won't be expecting us to try for a bustout, and . . ."

"But how?" Pinto cut in, adding, "Seeing it's just plain impossible?"

Elmo said, more thoughtfully, "Hold on, he never said we had to take the greasers along, did he?"

Seth said, "I did. We all go or we all stay. Before you give your fool self a big hug for being so clever about the seven of us having riding stock to spare, I'd best advise you I have a few tricks up my sleeve. You go ahead and bust out by yourselves if you've a mind to. That might give me and the other human beings an even better chance as the Indians chase you whilst we ride another way."

Elmo retracted, "Nobody said nothing about splitting up with Lord knows how many Apache tear-assing after us, boy. You say you've got a trick, a *horse* trick, neither me nor them Apache might know?"

Pinto scoffed, "They ride fast and far on them New Jersey dairy farms, boss."

Seth nodded pleasantly, and replied, "As a matter of fact, we had way more fences to jump back home than I've seen so far out here, and when they only give you one pony to ride you learn to take good care of it."

Pinto snickered, and said, "Next thing you'll be calling yourself an old top hand with a fine cutting horse for every day of the week."

Seth shook his head, and replied stubbornly, "I just got done saying I had to make due with my one all-purpose plug, and that's the point I'm trying to make, if only someone around here would listen. I'm not ready to take on any of you boys in a roping contest yet, but as far as plain old horsemanship goes, I'd say a heap of cow hands and cow ponies are downright spoiled. I'll allow herding unfenced beef cows calls for some dashing about with a change of mounts most every day, but what does that teach a man about horses, even when you look at the critter as you're getting on or getting off?''

Elmo frowned, and said, ''Make your point, old son. All of us know how to ride or we'd have never wound up out here so far from town.''

Pinto added, ''Damned A! I've been getting on and off of cow ponies at least as long as you've been walking, Jersey Lilly!''

Seth shrugged, and said, ''Mostly letting the wrangler in charge of the remuda worry about the sort of shape it may or may not be in. Like I said, you learn a few things about the species when there's nobody but yourself to water it, feed it, curry it, and when it's sick, nurse it back on it's feet.''

He saw from the thoughtful glances they exchanged that he'd scored a point. He added, ''It's not like I'm a licensed vet, you understand, but I know a thing or two about simple horse doctoring, and there's an old horse-trading trick I've been curious about ever since it was pulled on poor old Uncle Aaron at the county fare. A city slicker from East Orange sold him a frisky colt that turned into a worn out eight- or ten-year-old by the time he'd ridden it home from the fairgrounds. Oom Tromp, a sly old Dutchman up our road a piece, knew right off how it had been done.''

He shot a canny look of his own at Pinto, and added, ''You likely know how to turn an old plug into a frisky race horse for at least a few hours, too. Don't you, cowboy?''

Pinto looked uncomfortable, and said, ''Well, sure, I

know you can dope a horse up to run faster than it might want to on its own.''

"With what?'' asked Seth, innocently.

Elmo silenced Pinto with a warning look, and said, "You tell us, if you're all that smart. What have you got and where did you get it? Have these Mexicans got some horse dope I don't know about?''

Seth said, "They don't know about it either. Gordo's afraid we don't have the horseflesh to outrun them Apache. So I suspicion he never bought a frisky colt at the Essex County Fair neither.''

Elmo scowled, and insisted, "Get to the god damned point, boy!''

Seth shook his head, and replied, "Not hardly. I'd rather feel wanted than backshot. So I reckon I'll just keep a few things to myself till we've all agreed on a few things, my way.''

Pinto asked, "What's the deal then?'' But Elmo Dawson told him to shut up and turned back to Seth.

"Before anybody tries to dictate any terms around here, I'd like to make sure I savvy his offer. Is it your contention you can doctor all our ponies some way so's they'll have no trouble leaving them Apache ponies way behind?''

Seth answered cautiously, "*Way* behind may be asking too much, seeing some of our party will have to ride double. But most of the stock we have to work with starts out with some edge over your average Indian pony. You know why both the Pony Express and U.S. Cavalry ran circles around horse Indians in their glory days, of course.''

Elmo snorted, "Yeah, yeah, everyone but the writers for Ned Buntline's magazine knows Indians ride unshod stock they stuff with grass and tree branches, even when they ain't beating all the spirit outten 'em. I don't think much of the way greasers break in riding stock neither, if you want to know the truth.''

Seth admitted he knew next to nothing about the Hispanic vaquero who'd taught the anglo buckaroo the western beef industry, but added, "Any of these Mex folk who
still need riding lessons will surely get some betwixt here
and safer surroundings. As long as nobody falls off it
won't much matter aboard faster mounts. I'm pretty sure
I can doctor our stock to outrun any more natural pony
for at least the first five miles. Anyone still chasing us
after a run like that will likely be way out ahead of his
pals, and it ain't as if I advocate leaving all our guns behind."

Elmo Dawson pursed his lips and decided. "I don't
reckon I want to be left behind either. So what's the deal
you had in mind, old son?"

Seth said simply, "For openers we forget about back-
shooting anybody around here but Indians, and let's make
that Apache Indians while we're at it."

Elmo smiled thinly, and said, "I've noticed some of
Gordo's boys look like the stork meant to drop 'em down
the smoke hole of a tipi. But I'll agree we've got enough
on our plate with just the Apache if you'll answer me just
one question about this damned old gold mine here."

Seth shook his head, and said, "Who might or might
not own it, in the end, ain't near as important as all of us
getting out of here alive. You say you made a title search
and satisfied yourself the claim had been abandoned. Miss
Felicidad and Gordo say otherwise. Since I'm not even a
lawyer, let alone a mining court judge, I'm keeping an
open mind on all that. You can take her to law or vice
versa once all of us make it back to more civilized parts.
Agreed?"

Elmo glanced at the gaping mine adit beyond Seth, asking, "What's to stop the infernal Apache from destroying
the property either way? Do we leave it to their mercy?"

Seth said, "Nothing. They'll likely loot and burn everything they feel up to looting and burning. They didn't even enter the mine itself the last time they had the chance. If they do this time, so what? You were toying yourself with the notion of caving this adit in and just digging it out again after the dust and disputed ownership had some time to settle.''

Elmo looked away, ears red, to say, "Let's agree I was only toying. What's to stop someone else entire from claiming everything here as his own with neither us or that Mex gal here to argue about it?''

Seth chuckled dryly, and replied, "They call themselves Na Déné. We'll naturally tell the army they're here instead of wherever in hell the army's been searching for 'em. But by the time the army has 'em out of here you and Miss Felicidad will be suing each other for the record, and no matter which one wins, the courts won't be about to recognize any claims filed one day later, see?''

Elmo must have. He said, "Deal!" and when Seth held out his palm Elmo spat on his own right hand and slapped hard and wet to seal the bargain, adding, "Now tell us how we get our ponies to run faster than anything the Apache might have to ride after us with.''

Seth might have. He knew he was going to have to by suppertime if any of them were going to make it out alive. But just then a rifle squibbed way above them, and when they all looked up they saw the kid posted on the rimrocks as a lookout dancing about as if he'd been caught barefoot on hot coals. Pinto knew just enough Spanish to decide all that yelling from up yonder involved a bunch of riders, a big bunch, coming down the valley from the north.

Elmo frowned, and said, "We come through the ridge to the east further south. If they ain't army or more Indians, there must be a pass we missed on our own way in.''

Pinto said, "Caballeros gringo means riders like us, and that's what the greaser keeps calling 'em.''

Seth suggested, "Must be dozens of ways in and out through that maze of worn-down ridges. How they got here ain't half as important as where they're headed and what they want."

He started to head for the mine adit. Then he spied young Jose running up the slope toward them, yelling fit to bust. When Jose said he had to tell La Patrona and Gordo a mess of strangers had dismounted to form a skirmish line just north of the camp, Seth pointed at the adit, turned back to Elmo and the cook, and quietly suggested, "We'd best go have a look." When Elmo said he didn't like the looks of this at all, Seth could only reply, "That's what I just said."

Seth and the six Anglos he'd ridden out of Deming with were already forted up behind the watering troughs and horizontal poles along the north side of the camp corral when Gordo and a corporal's squad of his own armed men crawled through the dust churned up by the edgy ponies to join them. When Gordo asked what was up, Seth told him to see for himself. So the burly Mex removed his big sombrero for a cautious peek over the watering trough.

What he saw, beginning at say four hundred yards up the valley, was an east-west and spread-out line of eighteen dismounted and hunkered-down gents wearing mostly Stetson-brand hats and packing Winchester-brand repeaters as they, too, seemed content to wait and see what happened next. The ponies they'd ridden until recent were bunched by the stream another hundred yards out of easy rifle range. Seth told Gordo, "I make it an even two dozen ponies. So they got about six pals tending their remuda that we can't see from here."

Gordo growled, "I can count. So can Apache. Since those cabrones are not under attack at the moment, Los Indios must have ridden on in search of easier prey, no?"

Seth said, "Unless they're as puzzled as we are. You don't see any of us blazing away, and that don't mean we ain't here. The Indians have even more reason than we do for suspecting more tricks from our side, and anyone can see that those old boys out there, whoever they may be, can't be on the Indians' side."

Felicidad Robles came striding across the corral in the riding habit she'd changed to, calling out to them for answers they weren't at all sure about. So as Gordo yelled, "Pero no, mi Patrona!" Seth yelled, "Damn it, duck!" and when that didn't work either, he just jumped up, ran over to grab her, and threw them both to the dust, hissing, "That was dumb as hell, even for a she-male!"

She replied in a torrent of remarks that made Gordo blanch and a couple of the other Spanish speakers huddled behind the watering trough cross themselves. But by the time Seth had dragged her into line with them and let her have a safer look-see from cover, it was her turn to make the sign of the cross and ask, less imperiously, who on earth they could be and what on earth they might want.

Elmo Dawson, on her far side, said, "Only one way to find out. I got a white pocket kerchief if you got the nerve, Jersey Lilly."

Seth shook his head, and said, "I got the nerve. I just ain't dumb as some might hope. They must want to talk to us, or they'd have rid around us by this time."

Elmo insisted, "Meanwhile the hour grows late, and Lord knows how many Apache are observing this standoff with considerable amusement."

Seth shrugged, and said, "That's their beeswax and none of my own. I forget which general said it, but he must have lived through the war where he warned never to break cover when you didn't have to. So you go see what they want if you just can't stand to wait. I'll be proud to cover you from here."

Elmo tried. "Pinto?"

But the cook said, "I never thought the day would come when I'd agree with a dairy farmer about anything, but you know what they say about wisdom from the mouths of babes, boss."

They were saved from further argument by one of the Mexicans calling out, "Mirar!" They looked at a trio of strangers headed their way under a fairly white flour sack the one on their right was holding aloft on a crooked mesquite branch.

Fair was fair, so Seth stood up, exposing himself at least from the thighs up. Gordo hesitated and followed his lead. When Felicidad gathered her legs under her to follow suit, Gordo begged, "Tardar un momento, por favor!" and Seth told her, "Let's make sure they ain't outlaws before we let 'em see even an ugly gal on our side, Miss Felicidad."

She started to ask why, then murmured, "Oh," with a becoming blush.

Elmo Dawson got up instead, saying, "Hey, I know that tall one with the plaid shirt and silver conchos down his fandango pants. He'd be old Gus Hudson. Used to be a lawman over in Lincoln County. Raises stock in the Cooks Range north of Deming these days."

Then he took off his hat to wave it, calling out, "Hey, Gus! Gus Hudson! It's me, Elmo Dawson, and what are you doing up here in the Hatchets, you old cow thief?"

The three who'd been coming in cautiously started walking faster with the one Dawson knew in the lead as he called back, in as jovial a tone, "Looking for cheap remounts. Had I known they let you as well as Apache run loose in these hills, I'd have stayed home, Elmo. But just don't ask me to play cards with you again, and I might let you off this time."

The easygoing banter had inspired Felicidad and everyone else to rise to their feet. As they did so Gus Hudson's smile grew less certain. He ticked his hat brim politely at the Mexican girl, but growled, "You out to change your luck, Elmo?"

Dawson said, "These folk are all right, Gus. Last night we all fit Apache together."

Hudson looked relieved, and said, "Oh, that's better. They told us back at the county seat about yet another band of Mex Apache sneaking up from the Sierra Madre to take advantage of things, and you know what they say about Mangas Colorados dressing his band up like regular, ah, Spanish gents on occasion."

Seth said none of the Nedli or Mescalero they'd tangled with to date had been killed wearing pants or even hats. Dawson introduced Hudson to him and the others. Felicidad dimpled up at the husky gent to tell him her place was his place, Mexicans understanding such polite words weren't to be taken too literal, so it was Gordo who got to ask just what Hudson and his private army were doing up here so far from their own range.

Hudson answered easily, "I told you before, hunting saddle-broke mounts as don't have owners no more. With Apache foreign and domestic blowing military and civilian riders outten the saddle every chance they get, it's a heap safer to be born a horse than a human in these parts, so . . ."

"Wild Indians always leave stray stock in their wake," Elmo cut in, adding, "You'd best get your round-up crew in outten their rifle sights, Gus. For up to now we've seen more Apache in these parts than any other sort of animals. To tell the truth we were just now talking about making a break for it. But with this many gun hands on tap, I doubt they'd dare to try again."

Gordo started to kick up a fuss. But Felicidad hushed him in Spanish and agreed in English that it made simple sense for all Christian folk to stick together in the face of heathens. She said there was grass and water for ten times the number of ponies they had between them, and that the corn meal and beans on hand ought to keep everyone going at least to November. Hudson laughed, said, "There you go, ma'am. If Geronimo holds out till September, I mean to write nasty letters about the army to the newspapers."

He sent the kid who was holding the truce flag back to gather all his other followers before he rolled over the corral fence as if to get more cozy with Felicidad and her followers, explaining, "Things looked bad for wicked old Geronimo last I heard in town. General Miles got called back to Washington to explain how come he's so slow at rounding up the red rascals this summer. So with Head Scout Sieber stove up and Miles too far off to confuse his troops we may see the end of it any minute now."

Felicidad suggested they all head for some shade and a sit-down with cake and coffee. But she asked Hudson to explain his odd words further as they all headed back into camp, save for a couple of Mex kids detailed to go on guarding the remuda and the Anglo hand Hudson left to steer the rest of the boys to some coffee once they had their ponies corraled with the others.

Seth wasn't sure why he felt so annoyed when Gus Hudson offered his arm to Felicidad, and she took it. He found himself walking behind them next to Gordo. When the burly Mex saw he'd been caught glaring at the back of Hudson's shirt, Seth had to smile sheepishly, and murmur, "Great minds run in the same channels."

In front of them, Hudson was expanding on his own notions of Indian fighting. Seth had to admit it sounded as if the sort of handsome loudmouth might know. Hudson explained, "I don't know whether career officers know they're doing it or not, but I do know they just hate to end the game entire now that there's barely enough wild Indians to keep it going. The opposition newspapers have been accusing General Miles of giving the red pests more sporting chances than they deserve, too. Be that as it may, whilst old Miles is on the carpet back east the troops have been left in the care of their regimental surgeon, with young Tom Horn acting as their head scout.''

Felicidad said that struck her as odd, since even a lady of the Mexican persuasion could see Miles must have had some higher-ranking combat officers he could have left in charge.

Hudson laughed, and said, ''Officers with more experience might lead the yaller legs the wrong way, ma'am. Would you want an underling rounding up your Indians on you whilst you was back east telling congress why you'd failed so far?''

She laughed, too. Then she sighed, and said, ''In that case we can't hope for any cavalry riding to our rescue until General Miles gets back from Washington, right?''

Hudson shook his head, and said, ''The best-laid plans of mice and men gang aft' aglae, which means don't leave greenhorns in charge if you don't want 'em messing up. Geronimo hit a cow outfit right after old Miles left and treated everybody he took alive just awful. So the sawbones left in command of the troops called in his junior officers and scouts, saying he was open to suggestions because no matter what they'd taught him about Indians in medical school, he just had to do *something*!''

Elmo Dawson, on the girl's far side, asked if that meant the troops were on the move, with or without their nominal commander leading them. Hudson nodded, and said, ''Better yet, Tom Horn's out in front, speaking Apache good as Al Sieber but less worried about the civil-service rules.''

Seth couldn't help but say, ''I met Tom Horn up a canyon one time. I thought I'd spotted him first, and he still got the drop on me. In all modesty I'd say he was pretty good.''

Hudson nodded but seemed to go on talking to Felicidad as he replied, ''He's the best, if we're talking about getting the drop on anyone, red or white.''

Felicidad asked what he'd meant by Horn not understanding the terms of his employment. Hudson explained, ''I suspicion he understands 'em, ma'am. Old Tom just don't care that the first rule of civil service reads something like Never-Put-Your-Fool-Self-Out-Of-A-Job. Happened to me and my pals up Lincoln County way half-a-dozen years ago when Billy the Kid and other survivors of the Lincoln County War provided full employment for as many deputies as wanted to sign on the county payroll.''

Elmo said, ''I remember all that excitement. Pat Garrett got The Kid at the Maxwell Spread in the summer of '81, right?''

Hudson sighed, and replied, ''July the fourteenth. I'll never forget it. For they fired me at the end of the month. Old Pat had put us all out of business with just two pistol shots, one of 'em missing The Kid entire!''

Seth had to laugh, too. Felicidad said, ''I am beginning to understand. What will the famous Apache hunter do if there are no more Apache to hunt, eh?''

Hudson allowed old Tom would likely find somebody else to hunt and Seth said he sure wished they could be sure the Indian troubles were over. Then he started to say something about their original plan to bust out. But Gordo nudged him warningly, and even though Seth had no idea why, he thought it best to bite his tongue for the moment.

By this time they'd made it to the east veranda of the main log building. Since the kitchen door opened on that side, their redheaded hostess only had to give a gentle holler. Then she told them to get comfortable, and the cake and coffee would be joining them any minute now.

Seth managed to sit next to Felicidad on the edge of the planking. The infernal newcomer, Hudson, plopped down on her far side as if she'd invited him, and told her, "Billy the Kid had a Mexican sweetheart called Deluvina. She buried him in one of her dad's shirts, five sizes too big for the little rascal, and made a cross for his grave with 'Duerme bien, Querido,' carved on it. You know what that means, of course, Miss Felicidad?"

She nodded soberly, but said, " 'Sleep well, Beloved.' Pero is not the way I heard the story. Was not Deluvina Maxwell the daughter of Pedro Maxwell himself?"

Hudson said, "We called him Pete. He was half Scotch and half Mexican, making pretty little Deluvina three-quarters your kind of folk. After The Kid gasped his last, with his head in her lap and her cussing out Pat Garrett considerable, they tried to clean the story up by saying she and The Kid were no more than friends, but I ask you, did that cross have 'Duerme bien, *Amigo*,' carved on it?"

Felicidad laughed. Seth didn't see what was so funny, even though he knew amigo meant friend. Feeling a mite left out, he said, "Hudson is a Scotch name, too, ain't it?"

Gus Hudson smiled easily, and replied, "Might have known a gent named Grant would catch me in the act. Would your folk have been Glen Spey or Glen Morriston Grants, pard?"

Seth blinked and had to think before he replied. "Glen Morriston, now that I study on it."

Hudson nodded knowingly, and said, "We was a branch of Clan Donald. That's how come I'm wearing this Mac-Donald tartan shirt I bought in El Paso last winter. I'm sure glad we weren't MacLeods in the old country. For

I'd hate to explain a tartan as noisy as that one to even a Mexican.''

This time it was Felicidad's turn to look as if she didn't think it was funny. But she managed not to look downright cross as she got back up to see what was holding up their coffee. As she left them alone for the moment, Hudson nodded after her, and murmured, ''Nice. Is any of that spoken for, or can any number of Scotchmen play?''

Seth glanced around to make sure they were talking privately before he replied. ''Never mind anyone's love life right now, damn it. Seeing you brought the subject up, this might be time for a gathering of the clans indeed.''

By this time some of the others who'd ridden in with Hudson were arriving to find their own places along the veranda. Hudson nodded soberly, and said, ''I got a lot of fair gun hands and twice that many guns on my payroll, Prince Charlie, but who are we rising against this time?''

Seth confided, ''I'm more worried about someone rising against us. Are you saying you didn't know about this mining camp when you started out for Apacheria?''

Hudson shrugged, and said, ''Know about it now. What are they mining here?''

Seth said, ''Gold, but that's not important next to getting out of this confusion alive.''

Hudson asked what was so confusing, adding, ''Betwixt you boys, my boys, and all them greasers, no Apache with a lick of sense is about to come anywheres near us, and we just agreed their days are numbered. So as I see it all we got to do is sit tight and wait till the army rounds the rascals up for us.''

Seth felt sure Elmo Dawson was listening in, even though the cuss was jawing with Pinto down at the far end of the veranda. But knowing he might never get a better chance, Seth confided, ''I'm not near as worried about

Indians hitting us from outside as I am a Glen Coe situation I'm braced for, here inside our lines.''

Gus Hudson frowned thoughtfully, and repeated, ''Glen Coe, Grant? You have to understand my family got off the boat some time ago. I had to ask which shirt was Mac-Donald when I bought it that time.''

Felicidad came back to join them. As they both rose to greet her she said the coffee would be on its way in a momento. Seth stayed on his feet as she and Gus Hudson sat back down. Neither asked why. Victorian manners allowed folk to heed the call to nature but didn't allow for asking why someone might or might not be headed for the facilities. So Felicidad just turned to Gus Hudson as if she was hanging on his every word while Seth strode off and, catching Gordo's eye as the burly Mex glanced up from his own lonesome seat, motioned for the Mexican to follow.

As soon as they were around the nearest handy corner, Seth turned to Gordo and said, ''I fear we're in a whole peck of trouble. Do you think you could get Miss Felicidad, Jose, and mayhaps some other smart English speakers in one place for me, sort of discreet?''

Gordo nodded, but growled, ''For why? Don't you trust that Hudson hombre either?''

Seth said soberly, ''Even less than I trust old Elmo, and I know for a fact *he's* no damned good. What say we all meet at the Robles cabin within the hour, and I'll tell you a tale of a Scotchman from Clan Donald who says he never heard about the Massacre of Glen Coe.''

Gordo stared back blankly. So Seth tried, ''Show me a MacDonald who never heard of Glen Coe, and I'll show you an Irishman who never heard of Cromwell or a Mexican who never heard of Maximilian and Carlotta!''

Gordo grumbled, ''Hey, those two killed a great many of my people, you know!''

Seth nodded grimly, and said, "Keep that in mind, and meet me at Miss Felicidad's as soon as you can manage without giving the show away!"

It was going on sunset, and none of the lamps inside were lit as Seth told Felicidad and the handful of Mexican men assembled in front of her cold fireplace, "Glen Coe is an unimportant highland valley and a legend grown more important with every telling since it happened way back in the winter of 1692."

"Was not so long ago," grumbled Gordo, who would have gone into the history of his own clan among the ruby crags of the Sangre de Cristo to the east if Felicidad hadn't told him to hush and let her hear about Escosia.

Following her drift, Seth said, "Scotland ain't important. Glen Coe ain't important, next to what happened there when old Ian McDonald of Glen Coe got too trusting."

He went on to tell them the simple horror story, used to scare highland children ever since, not because of the blood and slaughter or even the babies left to freeze to death in bloody snowdrifts, but because the poor Mac-Donalds had *trusted* the Campbell of Glen Lyon when he'd ridden in with his armed followers, assuring them the recent fighting was over and that all he and his lads were after was shelter from the bitter north winds off the nearby icy sea.

Seth had them all rapt as kids listening to a bedtime story as he skimmed over the poetic parts about the visitors waking up in the wee small hours to slit the throats of the hosts who'd just wined and dined 'em and put 'em to bed as honored guests. Hispanic laws of hospitality were close enough to evoke shudders without his having to go into all the grim details. So he told them, "My real point is that Gus Hudson quotes Robert Burns about mice and men, twits the poor MacLeods about their notoriously loud tartan, knows the difference between the words plaid and tartan, and even told me where my own clan hails from, yet he claims he never heard of Glen Coe?''

Felicidad frowned thoughtfully and asked how on earth the matter had ever come up in the first place. Seth explained, ''I was in a hurry and afraid of being overheard. So I used Glen Coe the way a Texan might evoke the Alamo in a tough Mexican saloon, no offense, as a short and easy way to get my point across. I'm glad I did. For had I said right out I was afraid some of the others planned something dirty, he might not have given himself away.''

''Given himself away about what?'' Demanded Gordo.

Seth insisted, ''Don't you see it yet? He tried to tell me he'd never heard of a gold mine up this way either. Half the Anglos in and about Deming must have known Elmo Dawson was recruiting an expedition to seek out and claim the Robles mine.''

''Pero cómo?'' Felicidad demanded, insisting, ''My family found the lode before any of us were born!''

Seth said, ''Let's not go into ancient history before we find out if we have any future left. Suffice it to say Gus Hudson just recruited himself a bigger bunch to trail Elmo and the rest of us to the claim and jump it. Finding it surrounded by Apache and already owned by Mexicans must have surprised him as much as it did us. But he seems to think faster on his feet, and that's not the only thing as makes him more dangerous than old Elmo. For just between us sneaks Elmo Dawson's got more greed than guts. If Hudson rode through the Lincoln County War on either side, he likely knows a thing or two about dirty gunfighting.''

Felicidad said she found it hard to believe such an ''Encanto'' cuss could be plotting to murder her in her bed.

Seth avoided Gordo's eyes as well when he muttered,

"He may well be planning a few exceptions for at least the first few nights. They say the Campbells didn't kill all the MacDonald gals right off. But, thanks to my catching his guilty conscience off base with mention of such matters, we're in better shape than the MacDonalds were when their house guests turned on 'em in the wee small hours."

Jose protested, "Pero, we have already let them in among us, like coyotes among the sheep!"

Gordo growled, "Is no problem. We make big fiesta, get them drunk, and slit their throats first, no?"

Felicidad sucked in her breath. Seth raised a hand to hush her as he told Gordo, "No. To begin with I could be wrong. Gus said he had to ask when he bought a shirt in his clan tartan and, even if I'm right, you can't just butcher old boys who haven't done anything to you yet."

Jose asked why not. Seth replied, "To begin with, as the Campbell of Glen Lyon found out at Glen Coe, everyone else winds up with a mighty low opinion of you. The swell trick he played on his old enemies got him a whole fresh set as soon as word got out about what he'd done. Glen Lyon only headed up one branch of the widespread Campbell clan, and none of the other Cambells wanted a thing to do with him once he'd disgraced their name along with his as Glen Coe. The royal court he'd been trying to please by wiping out the sometimes pesky followers of old Ian Mhor, or Big John, repudiated his dirty deed as premeditated murder whether they'd wanted Ian Mhor dead or not."

He nodded to Felicidad as he added, "I shouldn't have to tell any of you how a mess of Mexicans murdering Anglos in cold blood would sit with an Anglo grand jury, do I?"

She licked her pale lips, and asked him, "Whatever are we to do, then?"

He smiled crookedly, and told her, ''We treat 'em as friendly as they mean to treat us.''

Everyone there but Gordo seemed to think that a grand notion. Gordo grumbled, ''Easy for to say. More *difícil* for to do. If this Hudson is a gunfighter of experience he will not have ridden in with a band of mariposas for to back his grab for La Patrona's property, and few of our people could know as much about killing.''

Seth asked what mariposas might be, and when they told him they were butterflies, he chuckled, and said, ''I doubt your hardrock mining men are quite that flutter-some either, and we'll have surprise and Mr. Thomas Edison working on our side. So gather all around, and I'll tell you my plan.''

Robert Burns had been on the money about the plans of mice and men. Never having delegated authority before, he didn't know how wisely he might or might not be doing it when he decided to let folk who might know more than he did about some things use their own heads. Whether it was smart or dumb, he left it to Pablo to alert enough but not all of the Mexicans to the danger and how they were to respond to it if it turned out to be real. Gordo agreed there were some things the smaller children and more hysterical adults, male or female, might be better off not fretting about in advance.

Seth sent Jose back up to the battery box on the rim-rocks with detailed instructions indeed. Seth had to have someone who could understand every word in command of that post.

Jesus Garcia, their head wrangler, was awarded the chore of quietly cutting the mounts they might need into a separate corral he and his boys could throw together easily enough after dark. He looked insulted when Seth told him to make sure they were the best ponies, and that everyone who weighed more than fifty pounds rated his or her own now that they had so many to choose from.

When Felicidad asked what she could do to help, he told her they'd be using her kitchen, and that he'd be right back, hungry, as long as they needed a fire in the stove anyway.

Then everyone there but Felicidad fanned out through the camp to do their chores. Seth was on his way back to her cabin with the box of stuff he'd gathered by matchlight in the explosives shed when Big Dipper, the taller of the two spitters from Texas, recognized him in the tricky sunset light and stopped him, saying, "Been looking all over for you, Jersey Lilly. Pinto wants to know whether you're camping with us or mayhaps some pretty Mexican this evening, seeing your bedroll's still lashed so tight to your saddle."

Seth smiled thinly, and said, "Pinto surely is a curious cuss. I'd ask him why he's so worried about who I sleep with, but I'm afraid he might tell me."

Big Dipper laughed lightly, and replied, "He is too ugly for gals to consider, now that you mention it. What you got in that box, pard?"

Seth said, truthfully enough since the infernal box was wide open, "Dynamite and coyote bait. You can never spread too much of either in Apacheria with the sun going down, you know."

Big Dipper stared soberly down at Seth's load, and said, "Elmo and old Gus both say them Indians are long gone."

"You mean they've sort of put their heads together, planning for the future?" Seth asked dryly.

Big Dipper nodded, and replied, "Matter of fact, they've got pretty thick since Elmo told Gus about the gold mine here. Gus didn't know what these greasers was doing way out here afore Elmo told him."

Seth had a time staying poker-faced as he replied, "Oh,

that's right. That other bunch was only looking for stray ponies, deep in Apache country with the Apache on the war path. I got to get back to work now.''

Big Dipper offered to help. Seth kept his own voice desperately casual as he replied, ''Thanks, but I'd feel safer doing it by myself. Neither high explosives nor deadly poison are too safe to play with.''

Big Dipper allowed he'd heard as much, and they parted friendly, considering.

When he lugged the box up Felicidad's back steps and into her log cabin, he found rank had its privileges in Mexico as well. She'd made him a swell Denver with fresh eggs and green peppers in a cast-iron spider on her kitchen range from Pittsburgh. He put the box aside in the dry sink and hung his hat on a peg while he was at it, saying, ''It's on. If not for tonight some other night soon. I just heard Elmo's been buttering up to Gus Hudson. So all they have to work out now is the division of the spoils.''

She started to protest; it seemed a mite premature to divide a gold claim while the lawsome owner was still breathing. But she'd grown up in New Mexico Territory as a Mexican. So she just told him to eat his omelet, and then they'd talk about midnight murders.

He got to wash the Denver down with fancier coffee than usual, too, sweetened with white sugar and canned cow. But he was too fired up to dawdle over his late supper and asked her where they could put the crockery whilst he used her stove and dry sink.

She told him to just leave everything where it was for the chica, or housekeeper, who tidied up in the morning. Seth rose, smiling crookedly, and said, ''Let's hope she gets to wash dishes in the cold gray dawn instead of having to ride for her life with the rest of us. I need a pail of water and some pots to start with. Wasn't that a hand pump I just saw out back in the gloom?''

Felicidad nodded, but said, "I have an earthenware regadera with a tap, there, in that dark corner. See it? Maybe I should light more candelas now that it has gotten so dark outside, no?"

He said, "No. The dark may not be all that's wandering around outside." He glanced out, saw none of her bitty windows offered any possible peeping tom a clear view down into the dry sink, and lifted the box up on the drain board before he proceeded to roll up his shirtsleeves, saying, "I got to cook some dynamite. A double boiler would be safer, if you got one, if you know what one is."

She said she wore shoes, too, damn it, but seemed more curious about his odd notions of cooking than upset by his unintentional insult. As she hunkered down to rummage a nesting pair of pots from under the shelving between dry sink and stove, she calmly observed she'd never tasted dynamite, cooked for raw, and asked if he felt a few peppers would add or subtract from the flavor.

He said, "As a matter of fact, it's sort of sweet. At least the nitroglycerin in it is. You see, dynamite's just a mishmash of nitroglycerin and spongy clay as makes it harder to set off so it's safer to handle."

Felicidad just looked confused when he took the pots from her, ran water into one, and nested them in the dry sink. Her bemused expression turned to one of alarm as he calmly proceeded to bust up dynamite sticks with his bare hands and drop them into the dry inner pot as casually as carrots. When she accused him of a mad intent to blow them both to kingdom come, he shook his head, and told her, "I just said the clay mixed in with it made it almost impossible to set the stuff off without a cap."

He put the double boiler on the stove, choosing a spot where the boiling would be neither too soon or too extreme as he went on. "I'm not looking to render the nitro outten the clay because I aim to blow anything up. It ought to be safe enough to handle roughly again once we make pony treats out of it. By the way, I could use some sugar and bread dough, if you got it. Tortilla meal will do if you don't.''

She said she had both tortilla meal and some sour dough starter for white bread or pie crusts, if he was really loco enough to bake nitroglycerin pastry.

He said he wasn't ready for the dough yet, explaining, ''Don't have to bake it. Ain't sure I'd want to try. The notion is to whip up pony treats, each about the size of crab apple. They'll find both the sugar and nitro yummy, and the dough ought to hold it all together and help hide any taste of the strychnine. To tell the truth, I've no idea what strychnine tastes like. But it can't taste too strong, else neither rats nor coyotes would swallow so much of it, see?''

She didn't. She said, ''Let me see if I understand, Seth. You say that if those gringos attack my people, and my people win, we shall still have to ride for our lives because there won't be enough of us left for to stave off another attack?''

He moved down to remove the coyote bait from the box as he nodded, and said, ''Right. There's a chance we can hold 'em off. There's a chance they'll never attack at all. But if we wait until they do attack, and we see we can't hold 'em off, it'll sure be a stupid time to try for a bustout.''

She said, ''I understand that part. What I don't understand is why you wish to feed poison to the very mounts we'll be depending on!''

He said, ''Oh, that's easy. Pony treats laced with strychnine and nitroglycerin are an old horse-trading trick. A man can get killed trying it around a race track. Give some varmint enough strychnine and it contorts its fool self to death. But at milder dosages, say enough to kill a rat, fed to a critter big as a horse, strychnine's more like a strong stimulator. Docs still give a pinch of strychnine now and again to sickly humans suffering heart failure. It's sort of risky, of course. Getting a heart to hammer too hard can hurt it as much as its ticking too slow. That's where the nitro comes in."

He held the coyote bait up to the light, reading the directions printed on the label, as he explained, "When nitroglycerin ain't blowing more solid objects to bits it has a kinder effect on the heart and blood vessels of any critter as can get some down. Nitro by itself don't speed the heart, but it keeps a speeded-up heart from busting or even hurting. So given strychnine and nitroglycerin at the same time your average saddle bronc ought to be able to leave a derby winner in its dust, and I doubt any Indians in these parts are apt to chase us aboard derby winners."

She still looked dubious and asked how long the effect might last. He said, "Hard to say. I know of one poor simp who got a frisky pony all the way home from the county fair, say twenty miles, before he noticed he'd bought an old plug for way too much. It says here a teaspoon ought to do a rat, and that the flavoring's already added. That sounds about right for a pony you want more frisky than dead. I need another pot with a tad of water and that sour-dough starter now, ma'am."

She nodded and asked how many mighty odd pony treats he meant to make. He said, "Many as I can, of course. We got a heap farther than twenty miles to ride, and every rider will want extra ones to dope his pony on the trail."

She asked what would happen if someone ran out, or even worse, overdosed his or her mount. He didn't answer. The poor little thing looked worried enough already.

The moon was coming up fuller and even more orange that night, while Seth joined Jose and another kid atop the cliffs where it felt as if he and Felicidad had foiled that first attack a million years ago. Jose said a moon that wet could mean rain before morning and added that when it did rain in the summer in Apacheria it made up for all the dry times in between.

Seth allowed the local Mexican had to know more about the climate of New Mexico than he did, and added, "What I'm really worried about is them light bulbs dangling down the cliff shedding plenty of light if and when they're called upon to do so."

Jose said he knew what he was doing and held up the knot of bared wire ends as if that proved something. Seth said he'd had time to study on both the three leads involved and the mild shock one got while clamping them together bare-handed. He hunkered down to twist all three wires lightly but firmly together, explaining, "Right. Now all you have to do is pump that plunger like you're out to churn a whole ton of butter, and the lights north and south of the cleft will blink on and off automaticated. Everyone who was here last night will know what's going on. Strangers might be more confused. In either event a man who lets another sneak up on him in the dark when it's only dark half the time deserves to get snuck up on."

Jose grinned wolfishly in the moonlight, but asked, "What about the light on the far side of this rock, should we suspect any movement over to the east?"

Seth started to say Gus Hudson and his big gang were the more dangerous menace. But that wasn't true. So he felt for the right wire, found it by touch, and twisted it into contact with the others, saying, "There. Feed some juice from the battery box, and all three bulbs will flash. You can never have enough lights flashing with wild Indians and Anglos prowling about in the dark."

Jose asked if that meant the first bunch who'd ridden in

with him were all fair game should the dance begin. Seth grimaced, and decided, "No. Just men on their feet looking menacing in your direction. I just can't say how many who rode in with me are likely to pitch in or get pitched at. There's even the chance Hudson's bunch will think it easier to just blow everyone but themselves away. I'll see if I can find out before anything at all gets that noisy. Meanwhile, I got some goodies for both of you and, for God's sake don't bite into 'em before I explain just what they are and how they work."

They didn't. After he'd explained the half-dozen pony treats he'd issued each of them, Seth let himself down the cleft and, sort of wishing he didn't have to, drifted over to the too-big fire Pinto had built near the south end of the original mine layout. Gus Hudson and some of his own boys lounged near the fire against their saddles. Elmo sat more upright on an overturned bucket, while Pinto hunkered closer, poking at the coals around his coffeepot.

Elmo glanced up, nodded in a friendly enough manner, and said, "We was just talking about you, Jersey Lilly. Heard you might be staying under the roof of a sweet señorita instead of turning in with your old pals tonight."

Seth laughed louder than he really felt like laughing, and said, "Neither one of you get to have your wicked way with me tonight, no offense. I thought I'd take my Winchester up on the rocks and see how romantic the moonlight gets." He looked around with a puzzled smile before he added, "I don't see my saddle and bedroll, let alone my Winchester though."

Elmo hesitated. Then he stated softly, "That ain't your saddle or bedroll, boy. It ain't your Winchester neither. It's mine, bought and paid for, if you take my meaning."

There was only one way to take it. Seth took one step backward to clear an unknown person smoking quietly to his right as he said softly, "Might have known you'd fire me after I helped you get here instead of the other way around. Is that it, or do you want to get rid of me more personal?''

Elmo looked away, and murmured, ''I'm not armed, boy. Do you always dare your boss to a duel when you get fired for sassing him back?''

Seth snorted in disgust, and said, ''You ain't heard half the sass I could throw your way if I thought you gave toad squat about a white man's opinion of you. I take it you've told everyone here what I refused to go along with?''

Gus Hudson barely raised his voice as he smiled across the fire at Seth, saying, ''Leave me and mine out of this, if you know what's good for you, laddy buck!''

Seth nodded soberly, and said, ''That suits me fine. So seeing I ain't wanted here, I'll just say adiós to this other son of a bitch.''

Gus Hudson shook his head and rolled away from his saddle to sit up straighter, saying, ''We don't want you to leave us just yet, Grant. Why don't you just hunker down for some coffee with us. It's almost ready. Ain't that right, Cooky?''

Pinto didn't look at Seth as he murmured, ''Any minute now and it's real Arbuckle brand.''

Hudson said, ''There you go, laddy buck. We'll let you know when we want you to go telling tales out of school, see?''

Seth did indeed, but tried, ''Tales about what? What's going on here? Where are all the other boys, and just what might they be up to?''

Elmo nodded at Hudson and said, ''He likely knows, Gus.''

So Hudson sighed and rose to his feet with surprising speed as Seth saw that one to his right was uncoiling like a sidewinder at the same time, and timing, damn it, was nine-tenths of any quick-draw contest!

Seth knew that was what it was. Real gunfighters never hemmed and hawed like kids in a schoolyard before they went for their guns. So Seth went for his Schofield as he crawfished back from the light, sickly certain this was it, for though it all seemed to be taking place at the slow pace of a bad dream, his gun, and their guns, were on the way out and up through the glue-thick air. There was just no way he could aim at both, and Jesus which one should he be aiming at right now when both were throwing down at him, and . . .

The Edison bulbs flashing on up above surprised and dazzled them more than they did Seth, and in that fraction of a second it took a man to gasp and swing his gun muzzle up instinctively the one to Seth's right died on his feet with a bullet in his brain.

Gus Hudson fired higher than he'd meant to, too, as Seth threw himself backwards to land in the dirt on his back and roll farther away as the light bulbs flashing through all the gunsmoke, so far, made Hudson miss with his second shot as well.

Then Seth fired Hudson's way from his prone position and either hit him or inspired him to duck like hell on the far side of that fire. Seth had no idea who fired the carbine from the darkness to his rear and blew Pinto away from his fire with the port-wine birthmark on his ugly face looking more like cherry jam.

Seth got Elmo Dawson as the sneak-to-the-last rose from his bucket with the six-gun he'd been holding all this time in his lap. As Dawson went down one of Hudson's other boys rose with both hands in the air, shouting, "I give! I give!" only to catch a couple of bullets with his belly at once while somewhere in the night some Mex kid let fly that mocking rooster laugh his kind delighted in.

Seth rolled farther from the firelight and sprang to his feet. He ran over to an ore tram parked near the log side of a shed and crouched in the flickering shadows to reload before forging on. He knew the layout of the mining camp. He knew where he was going. It was still confusing as hell with those electric bulbs flashing on and off to afford alternate glimpses of blurred motion and pitch blackness. Each flash left an afterimage that might not be there the next time the lights winked on. You had to fire at the memory of a target instead of the target if you meant to hit anything at all. From all the smoke and gunfire Seth figured he couldn't be the only one doing it. He held his fire when the image of Little Dipper flashed on, yelling, "I'm on your side!" But the next time the lights flashed the Texan was on his knees spitting blood instead of Rooster brand snuff, and neither of them would ever know who'd killed him, for Seth had moved on before Little Dipper got done dying.

He didn't know who might be winning, but he did know the fight had started earlier than either Elmo or Gus could have planned, and he knew where he'd be heading right now if he was Gus. So he tried to get there first. Gus Hudson was banging on Felicidad's back door as Seth ran in as far as the backyard pump, drew a bead on Gus, and yelled, "Drop that gun and grab for some stars, Hudson!"

Hudson did neither. It seemed impossible, but it likely always did when a less-experienced gunfighter gave a real pistoleer any break at all. Seth was sprawled in the dust with an armpit filled with molten lava and a right arm numb and useless as an empty leather sleeve by the time he figured, "Shit! I'm shot!"

He was trying to do something, anything, about it in a dreamlike state when the man who'd just shot him became an inky black figure outlined in bright muzzle blast. Felicidad, not about to open her door, fired both barrels of her dead dad's ten-gauge through it to blast the life out of Hudson with sharp cedar splinters and number nine buck!

As she threw open what was left of her door, sobbing, "Querido! A dónde es?" Seth yelled, "Get back inside, and keep your head down!"

She slammed what was left of the door, as if that would do a lick of good now. Seth found himself laughing, despite the little white stars pinwheeling in midair over Gus Hudson's face-down smouldering remains. It felt even worse when he grabbed the water pump with his left hand and hauled himself back up. Felicidad's back steps seemed a hundred miles away. The dead body between him and there squished funny when Seth walked right over it. He wasn't about to go around. His right arm was full of pins and needles now, and he seemed still to be gripping his fool six-gun. He wasn't sure how you let go of one with your hand dangling so dead at your side. He didn't think he ought to throw his gun away right now in any case. From all the noise and flashing that was still going on, it hardly seemed the fight could be over yet.

He reeled up the spinning steps, and Felicidad opened up again to haul him inside and drop him in front of the stove. She opened the stove to shed ruby light on his condition and got even more excited when she saw so much blood. But while she hadn't been raised to display a stiff upper lip about such matters, she'd been taught to do something pronto about gunshot wounds. So she tore off his bloody shirt and got cracking.

She began by cleaning him up a heap. Hudson's round had gone through the tender flesh of his inner arm, high enough to leave armpit hair in the wound, but it wasn't in truth as bad as it looked or felt. The numbness, already beginning to wear off, had been mostly caused by shock, and while he was still losing blood, the bullet hadn't torn through any major blood vessels, nerves, or tendons. As she polticed and bandaged him tightly above the biceps, Felicidad assured him he'd feel good as new in a few days.

She was also sure one of her late father's shirts would fit him if they left the top buttonholes agape. She even sponged off his bloody gun with the last of the water from that double boiler and asked if he'd like her to reload for him. So by the time Gordo joined them Seth was reloaded, reshirted, and ready for most anything that didn't take any real effort.

Gordo said, "We won, I think. Nine of our own are dead, counting two women and a muchacho who just wouldn't keep his head down. The others are all dead or scattered on foot. What do we do now? Los Indios have not been heard from so far this evening. They may not be out there any more, eh?"

Seth said, "We can't take the chance. We'll want to ride north, in the deep shade of the cliffs, before the moon rises high enough to kill that cover. So we'd best get everyone left over to the corrals and saddle up."

Felicidad protested, "Won't I look most foolish, abandoning all this property, if those Apache are no longer out there?"

He shook his head and insisted. "You'll still be alive, as well as beautiful. If the Indians are gone, you won't even lose another window pane by the time it's safer for you to come back. If there are Apache enough to really damage your property, you surely don't want your sweet hide in the vicinity at the time, see?"

Gordo said much the same in Spanish, and even though Felicidad was beautiful, she wasn't dumb. She looked around as if she never expected to see the already-gloomy interior of her cabin again, shrugged, and said, "Give me time to get my saddle gun and rain gear."

Gordo said he'd meet them over by the ponies. Seth said, "Hold on. You'd best take some more of these pony treats we cooked up earlier. It may take a few minutes to pep the horses up, and we surely don't want to ride out on slow stock.''

They didn't. Seth had in fact used a tad more strychnine than it took to set a pony's nerves a-tingle and speed its already-powerful pulse. So the ones cut from the remuda by Garcia were almost unmanageable, and by the time they'd all been bridled and saddled the narrow strip of dark shade between the cliff base and valley stream had gotten mighty skimpy.

Seth made Gordo repeat in loud Spanish how vital it was to keep together and out of the infernal moonlight as they made their dash for it. When they had most of the survivors mounted Seth, still afoot, turned to those around him, and said, ''Bueno, like us buckaroos say. Gordo, I want you to take the lead with all the women and children along with a few good men to guard 'em. Jose and me will follow as your rear guard. Praise the Lord I got the Winchester back with my saddle when we finally found it.''

Gordo frowned, and said, ''You are not in shape for to guard anything, and what if they have set up an ambush out ahead of us?''

Seth said, ''I'm in better shape to fire a carbine than I am to order frightened women and children about in Spanish. As to your second question, if the Apache are not only still out there but reading our minds, we're already dead and just too dumb to lie down yet. Our whole stunt hinges on the fact it sounds so dumb it may be smart. So move it on out, damn it, and if we're riding into an ambush, well, feel free never speak to me again.''

Gordo laughed, clapped Seth on the shoulder that wasn't shot up, and said, ''Mucho gusto, gringo. I think you are loco en la cabeza, pero I like you.''

Then he spun around to head for his own mount with surprising lightness.

Seth turned to Jose to ask what mucho gusto meant. He wasn't nearly as surprised to hear it meant "Good luck" as he was to see Felicidad still there in her black riding habit, her face shaded by the brim of her flat Spanish hat. He said, "I wanted you out front with the other noncombatants, Miss Felicidad."

She said, "Pooh, ask Gus Hudson who's a fainthearted woman around here. You need me with you if Jose here gets hurt. None of the others speak English, see?"

He said, "Not hardly. What if *you* get hurt?"

To which she demurely replied, "You will still have Jose. Don't you think we'd better mount up, caballeros?"

He had to agree. But as they strode side-by-side across the moonlit dust, he confided, "I liked it better when you called me querido."

She flustered. "Ay, que muchacho! Don't you men ever think of anything else? I was excited, not in love, when I thought you had been killed at my back door. Why did you call out to that other Casanova like that anyway?"

He said, "I couldn't just shoot knowing you were likely on the far side of that thin door. Hudson wasn't out to trifle with your charms as much as he was out to grab some cover and your gold claim at the same time. He figured none of us would risk shooting after the two of you in the dark as you rode out together."

She gasped, "My God, and once we were well out of range . . ."

"He might have just killed you outright," Seth soothed, adding, "I doubt any Apache as catch us will. So should we run into any fire, and you ain't the first one hit, make sure you just keep going without looking back!"

They'd made it over to the pony line by now. The Mexicans trying to hold 'em steady were having a time. Seth started to help Felicidad mount a big, black gelding. She told him not to be silly, and in truth he'd have had more trouble getting aboard the barb who knew him better when it wasn't doped if Jose hadn't given him a last boost.

Gordo and the main party had already lit out, unseen but hardly unheard as they moved north along the inky ribbon of darkness at a flat run. Seth twisted in the saddle to make sure all the ones with him were ready to go. As the last Mexican youth vaulted aboard his dapple gray, Seth yelled, "Vamanos!" not really certain it meant "let's go!" but it must have, for as he spurred his barb forward everyone else came with him, and thanks to the strychnine and nitro the ponies had just been fed, they came out of the corral moving like spit on a hot stove!

Seth forgot his wound in the sheer delight of tearing through the night in the saddle of a really sudden horse moving flat out. For while a lope called for concentration on one's breathing and a trot was downright uncomfortable, the rapid hoofbeats of a moving mount canceled the ups, downs, and sideways to offer as smooth or smoother a ride than a slow walk. The sense of motion and the wind in his face made him want to laugh and yell out loud.

He didn't, of course. There were times for rebel yells or vaquero crows, and this wasn't one of 'em. Like those riding with him, he had to trust the superior night vision of his mount as they tore along the base of the cliffs, leaping or dodging a fallen boulder from time to time. For the contrast betwixt the route ahead and the moon-silvered slopes to their left made the shadows even inkier.

But the dotted line raising moonlit dust up the slope and out ahead could be made out plain enough, and Seth only snorted in disgust when Jose, right behind him, shouted, "Mirar! Mirar! Los Apaches!"

Seth yelled back, "Keep going. They can hear us, but

they can't see us and, from the way they're aimed, they're confused by the echoes of our hoofbeats!''

Jose just babbled in Spanish. Felicidad's voice sounded as scared but more sensible as she relayed Seth's orders, only to demand, once she'd done so, whether it seemed prudent to keep going when it looked as if the Indians would make it to the shade ahead of them.

He grunted, ''Not if we cut the bull and, damn it, *ride*! They're only riding human horseflesh, and if we get through the gap a tad ahead of 'em . . .''

They did. Some of them at any rate. The Indians had been drawn down from their positions along the timbered ridges to the west by the sounds of Gordo's advance party. They'd been bewildered by both the echos and the direction of the second clatter of steel-clad hooves on sandstone. So they rode into the ribbon of blackness blind but, being Na Déné, willing and able to go for broke.

Someone shouted ''Dikahahahahah!'' which hardly sounded Spanish, as gun muzzles flashed all about, and Seth's recklessly running barb crashed into a scrawnier pony and spilled its spitting and cussing rider. He heard Felicidad's feminine voice let fly one of those taunting vaquero crows, and when it was drowned out in a fusillade of gunfire, he could only hope that had been mostly her doing all that shooting.

His own pony flew over a big boulder with him, and he almost spilled as they came down on the far side, a mite off balance and running sort of funny. He tried to haul the Winchester from its saddle boot and found he couldn't on the run, with his right arm still so weak. He seemed to be ruining Don Hernan's shirt, too, unless that was one hell of a lot of sweat running down his arm now.

His barb couldn't say so, but Seth knew from the way it was running that it had been hit. Thanks to the strychnine coursing through its veins and the nitro keeping said veins from bursting, the doped pony still ran faster wounded than most could in better shape. Seth found he could get out and handle his six-gun. He was drawing his weapon when, less than a mile on, without any warning, his mount went limp and useless as a big wet feather mattress under him, and he was sprawled in dusty grit with some other dumb son of a bitch riding over him in the dark.

Fortunately horses never willingly trust their weight on anything squishy as a human body, so Seth only lost his hat to a grazing hoof and recovered to put it back on as he rose to his feet, spitting dust as he stared back into the dusty darkness, gun in hand but weak of knee and trying not to cry as he bared his teeth and sort of sobbed, "All right, you bastards, let's just see if one of me is worth five of you!"

He laughed despite himself, and added, "Make that four," as he recalled what everyone said about saving that last round for the sweet repose of one's own poor soul. Then he heard hoofbeats behind him, whirled, and almost blew Felicidad Robles off her big gelding before he recognised her black outline against the starry sky behind it. She was having a tougher time spotting him, and so she called out "Quién es?" and raised the gun in her own right hand before he could answer, "It's me, afoot. They got my pony, and I thought I told you to just keep going, girl!"

She holstered her weapon and reached her free hand down to him, saying, "We'll have to ride double." When he protested it was a swell way for them to die together, she answered simply, "So be it. I'm not leaving without you."

He holstered his Schofield, hauled himself up behind

her to ride pillion, and growled, "Women. We can't live with 'em and they won't let us live without 'em."

She spurred her big gelding forward with a merry laugh, considering. He told her to just shut up and keep going, adding in a softer tone, "Let the Indians guess where we might be. We're for certain way behind the others now."

She said, "I know. They got Jose and poor old Jesus Garcia. I hope they're both dead."

Then it was too tough to talk with the gelding loping under them like that. Felicidad knew she had to let it just lope, carrying two, no matter how many pony treats they fed it.

Fortunately the long-legged brute had a mile-eating stride, and between them they were packing plenty of the big dough balls they'd made. When she stopped a couple of miles on to feed their mount, Seth warned her, "Not yet. I don't know the dosage that's safe, and we'll be in a real fix if we lose this mount as well."

She asked, "Won't we be in worse shape if those Indians catch up with us?"

He said, "Keep going. So far you've been doing fine, and this good old pony will let us know when it can't lope on without more stimulation."

She glanced back the way they'd just come, and protested, "I can't tell if we've lost them or whether they're right on our tail. What if we were to cut across the water to continue by moonlight. That way we could see how many and how fast they may be following, no?"

He answered, "No. They'd see us for certain, and if they went on hugging the cliff like so they might even get ahead and cut us off again, see?"

She did and said he sure was smart for an easterner. Seth was too polite and the gelding's long-legged lope was too jarring for him to quietly ask how often your average westerner got chased by Apache. He was commencing to feel it didn't really take all that much experience to qualify as an old Indian fighter. You got it right the first time or you just didn't get older.

So they loped on, and on, and by the time he did let her stop to rest their mount and feed it another pony treat the moon was so high they could see back along the base of the cliffs for at least a quarter-mile.

Seeing nothing but their own settling dust, Felicidad heaved a sigh of relief, and said, "I think we've outdistanced them."

He could only say, "Maybe. You'll be right if they don't catch up and wrong if they do. Either way, it looks like we'll have the whole infernal band to ourselves from here on."

The moon had set, and sunrise was threatening by the time they came to the deep twin ruts of the east-west stage coach trace through the Hatchets. The sky above looked sort of like a big gray blanket, and from time to time thunder muttered somewhere below the horizon. They dismounted by tacit agreement to water and poison her pony some more before riding on. Felicidad was sure Gordo and the others would have followed the coach trace east, since it led straight in to the county seat of Deming. Seth stared down at the hoofprints running both ways, and decided, "That's the way I'd read it if I was a really stubborn Apache. Deming must still lie twenty miles from here, and we'll be lucky if your mount can carry the two of us much farther at a walk. There's no way we're going to get another full gallop out of him without killing him."

She nodded, but said, "We must have left those Indios far behind, and are there not some stage stops between here and Deming?"

He shook his head, and said, "Deserted. For the same reasons I'd hate to defend anything with an inflammable

roof against an attack, way out in the middle of nowheres.''

He stared thoughtfully the other way, not able to see all
that much in the murky, predawn light. He still said, ''Our
best bet has to be Lordsburg, over on the west slope of
the divide. It's only a few miles farther, and the Indians
might not expect us to go for those extra miles, even without thunder on the mountains.''

She protested, ''I should think not! Lordsburg is more
than ten miles further, on the map. Through these mountains is much farther because you have to count up and
down as well as twist and turn.''

She saw that seemed to make him smile. So she added,
''Even if it was not so far, there will be more snow than
lightning to worry about up along the divide. Both of us
are dressed for summer riding, not for riding through a,
how you say, blizzard?''

He nodded, and said, ''So much the better. Them Indians ain't even wearing pants. I lost my tarp along with
everything else I wasn't wearing when they spilled me way
back yonder. But you got your slicker as well as your
bedroll tarp, and we can always bundle up if it gets really
cold, can't we?''

She laughed despite herself, and said, ''I might have
known you'd think of a trick like that. We'll talk about it
when and if we really have to. I'd feel safer under a tarp
with a cold hombre than a hot one.''

He said that sounded fair and started up the coach trace
to the west afoot to lead their pony further from their
pursuers even as they rested it. She strode beside him in
step, not asking why. He liked gals who could think for
themselves without asking all sorts of fool questions. It
was too bad she was a greaser, even if she was a white
one. Of course his dad had been a papist and Mom's Calvinist kin had gotten over it in time. But what the hell,

neither he nor even she was likely ready to settle down yet. If they had been, she owned a gold mine, and he wasn't sure how he'd ever get all the way on to Tombstone yet.

They'd gone over a shallow rise through a gunsight notch in a lava dike and paused to remount with the trail ahead downhill and the gelding hopefully rested. But as he was boosting Felicidad into her saddle it felt as if a bodacious wad of warm spit had landed on his hat brim. Felicidad must have been hit by another. She sighed, and said, "Acelerar! Is starting to rain, and once one's clothes get wet they stay that way in weather such as we are about to be afflicted with!''

She was right. For though she wore her oilcloth slicker and he was wrapped in her tarp before it really got to coming down fire and salt, the few really wet spots on his shirt stayed sticky as a snail's belly button. Their mutual mount, catching all the downpour neat with its steaming hide, was inspired to lope down-slope and even trot up-slope as they forged on for the continental divide in the still-murky light, wondering how long it would rain like this before the damned sun got to shining the way it was supposed to by now.

As a matter of fact, it rained until almost noon and then, seeing they'd gotten to higher and cooler parts of the Hatchets, the rain gave way to snow, wet snow, mixed with thunder and lightning.

The only thing to be said for such freaky weather was that not even the Na Déné breed of Indians was likely to be out on a day like this if they didn't have to be.

Felicidad agreed when he told her he'd thought they had really awesome thunderstorms in the New Jersey hills back home. She said she found it spooky when lightning siz-zled nearby among the swirling snowflakes, too. By this time there was tall timber, mostly pine, to either side of the coach trace, whether rising or dipping. Their gelding was acting more spooked than frisky as the air around them filled with the mingled odors of wet snow, singed sapwood, and static electricity. Felicidad thought they ought to hole up beside the trail, where it dipped, until the storm blew over. He asked how long these summer storms they had out here might last.

She answered, "Quíen sabe? It can be dry as a mummy's smile or storm all through July and August in this corner of New Mexico."

He grimaced, and said, "July ain't barely started. So we'd best keep going."

They tried, even when she protested they were more likely to be struck by lightning on the ridges. He knew she was right, but there were ridges to cross over whether they kept going or turned back.

Some of the lightning strokes sizzled close enough to tingle all the hairs on both of them. But in the end it wasn't a stroke of lightning that killed the big gelding under their very rumps. As far as they could ever figure later, the poor brute just suffered some sort of heart attack and, in any event, dropped in the fetlock-deep snow as if it had been poleaxed.

As Seth helped Felicidad back to her feet she stared down in dismay at the still-steaming black hide of her dead horse, asking, "Now what?"

He said, "First we free your saddle gun, bedroll and canteens. Then we start walking. For as far as I can tell, we ain't even made it all the way to the top yet."

She muttered some indelicate-sounding remarks in her own lingo but was otherwise a sport about it as they trudged onward and upward through the swirling and at least now drier snow.

They'd have made better time in their soaked-through riding boots if the snow hadn't settled deeper as well as drier at this altitude. As it started spilling in over the tops of their boots, Felicidad insisted, "We're never going to be able to walk all the way to Lordsburg suffering quemado del hielo. I think you call it bites of frost."

He smiled wistfully, and said. "Close enough and, to tell the truth, I feel cold all over."

They paused, and he stared about until he spotted two bushy junipers growing cheek by jowl a few yards off the trace. He pointed to them, and said, "If we both get under this tarp in the lee of them wind-busting junipers, we may get snowed in, but I doubt we'll wind up frostbitten."

She followed him as he broke trail through the even-deeper snow up the slope to drop the blankets he'd been packing dry under the tarp and spread it more invitingly.

Felicidad peeled off her slicker to spread as a ground-cloth, put the blankets atop it for now, and they were soon bundled snug as two bugs in her tentlike tarp. She snuggled close to him. She had no other choice. But when he put an arm around her, she warned him not to get fresco.

He said, "I ain't trying to get fresco. I'm trying to get warmo. Hold on. If I brace my back against this one springy tree, we can get comfortable sitting up. There ain't enough of this old tarp for the two of us to lie out flat."

She giggled and said that was no doubt just as well. But once he had them in a more braced-up position he noticed she seemed willing to lean her full weight against his left shoulder. It was just as well she was on that side. His right shoulder was starting to feel hot and throbsome, even though his arm and gun hand below the tight bandages was commencing to feel a lot more natural.

When he told her the bandage felt too tight now, she told him, "It can't be too tight before we get you to a real doctor. You could be in more trouble if your wound was not swollen and inflamed by this time. Deep wounds that

do not bleed or hurt much are the ones that kill in the
end.''

He told her she sure was a cheerful little thing, and the
next thing he noticed he seemed to be waking up with a
start.

It naturally roused her as well. She asked what was
wrong, and he said, ''Don't know. Didn't even recall dozing off. But then you never do, and we must have. So just
keep still, and let a man listen.''

She did. He thought at first the gray light shining
through the air slit they'd left in their tarp was just more
of the same gloom. But then he saw snow had caked in
the slit, and when he poked it out of the way with a finger
the sun outside was shining blindingly bright on a winter
wonderland even though it was pushing the Fourth of July.
He laughed, and said, ''Thunderation! We must have been
dozing under here for hours, and now we've turned into
one of them Eskimo igloos. The coach trace has been
buried good, too. But we'll likely be able to follow her,
and there must be a few hours sunlight left, so . . .''

''Wait!'' She protested, ''I have only now gotten comfortable, and if the trail is still covered deeply . . .''

''We're not too far from the divide,'' he cut in, adding,
''If you let me lead you over the worst part during this
break in the storm, I promise we'll hole up like this as
soon as it gets bitter again.''

She said that sounded fair. So he was about to toss their
snow-covered tarp aside when a gray jay bitched loudly
and fluttered its way through the trees down-slope.

Seth said, ''That jaybird must have been what woke us
up just now. Let's just hold the thought till we see what
has it so proddy.''

They did, even though it felt like forever before two
mounted Indians with their hair bound and faces painted
Na Déné slowly rode into view, staring cautiously about

as they loomed ever closer. Seth told Felicidad to shut up and not even breathe when she whispered, ''Madre de Díos! What they say about them being part bloodhound must be true!''

Seth figured it had been a lucky guess, given only two to choose from once they'd seen no steel-shod ponies had ever crossed that coach trace. With a little more luck the scouts would ride right past them. For the swirling snow had covered their footprints to this hidy-hole as well as the lump they made itself.

But eyes living as close to nature as theirs were less apt to dismiss landscape features as mere accidental flaws in Spider Woman's grand design. So even as he was explaining why he didn't want to fire the Winchester she was shoving at him, one of the Indians seemed to be staring right into Seth's eyes. When the Indian gave a birdlike chirp to his companion and pointed right at their snowed-in shelter Seth had no choice but to rise from it like a jack-in-the-box, blazing away with Felicidad's repeating Winchester until, as the roar of all that .44-.40 fire echoed away, the two Indians lay sprawled in blood-flecked snow, and Seth was running down to catch those damned ponies before they ran off!

It was easier than he'd feared. For horse Indians just hated to be left afoot and tended to loop the ends of their single reins around a wrist.

Both these boys had. So while the ponies spooked and rolled their eyes at him, Seth soon had them under control and clear of the dead men they knew better. As he led them up toward Felicidad she clapped her hands and said, ''Ay que linda! Now we do not have to walk all the way after all!''

He said, ''Grab your slicker and hold this Winchester for me whilst I boost you aboard this buckskin, bareback. I'll feed 'em some of our special treats now that we got the dosage figured out better, and with luck we'll be out of here before the others get here in response to them gunshots!''

She asked what about the tarp and blankets, and he almost snarled, ''Have you got wax in your ears, girl? If we get over the top ahead of the redskins it's a downhill run all the way on pepped-up ponies. If we don't, we still won't have any need for the extra weight. How many times do you expect me to cope with fighting men who know more about their trade than I do?''

They made it. It wasn't easy, but if the Indians followed them over the windswept and snow-covered continental divide late that afternoon, neither of them ever spotted them, even though Felicidad looked back often enough to turn into a pillar of salt, in Seth's opinion.

They paused at sunset long enough to water the captured Indian ponies at a mountain stream and rest all their bones until the moon rose high enough to light their way down the western slope of the Hatchets. Riding an hour and resting a quarter to half an hour in turn they crossed an ominously open stretch of chaparral by the last of the moonlight and got into the seat of Hidalgo County not long after sunrise.

Felicidad had the money, or at least the local credit, so as Seth put the jaded and now-sick ponies in the Lordsburg Municipal Corral, she ducked into the Western Union across from the Butterfield Station to get back in touch with her world.

As Seth was explaining their odd mounts to the hostlers at the corral, they were joined by an old, gimpy geezer wearing a faded pair of cavalry pants and spitting tobacco enough for the late Big and Little Dippers combined. He nodded at the listless-looking scrubs and said, ''Apache stock or I'm blind. No other nations braids their bridles like that. Where's you get 'em? Last we heard here the army had both Geronimo and Naiche pinned down with mountain guns a good many miles from here.''

One of the hostlers introduced the coot as an old army scout. Seth shook with him, and said, ''We brushed with Nedli, or maybe Mescalero, a good day's ride to the southeast.''

The old-timer stated flatly, ''Not Mescalero this year. Must have been Nedli. Understand Los Federales are out to solve their own Indian problem at the same time, seeing President Cleveland seems serious about it for a change.''

He spat, and added, ''Nedli never stay north of the border long. They don't know the country, and if the army don't get 'em the Papago will. Nobody fights Apache better than Papago.''

Seth said he didn't know much about Papago. The old timer told him, ''That's 'cause they're decent. You hardly never read about Injuns as ain't out to hurt no white folk. But if you knew Papago good as me, you'd sure be glad *them* old boys never go on the warpath agin' us!''

''Tough, eh?'' asked Seth. The old coot answered, ''Tough ain't strong enough a word. Every time the damn-fool army corners hostiles they make a new treaty with 'em and escort 'em back to some agency. Papago got more sense. It must have been a quarter-century ago Apache made the mistake of raiding the Papago. The Apache ain't forgot it yet. Them usually easygoing Papago chased 'em all the way back to the White Mountains and just kept lobbing arrows into 'em 'til every damn one who'd spilled a drop of Papago blood was in no shape to ever spill drop one of blood again!''

Seth said he'd never spill any Papago blood on a bet and took his leave of them to amble over to the Western Union. Felicidad met him out front, smiling, to tell him Gordo and most of the others had made it safely into Deming.

She said, "Better yet, the stage line's running again with army escorts, to make sure the mail gets through. There's a coach leaving this very noon, and I've gotten used to sleeping sitting up with you, so . . ."

"I don't have no business in Deming no more," he cut in, adding, "I only hired on with Elmo Dawson to get out of there before I could get in more trouble. I've kin waiting for me in Tombstone, if ever I can get there on the pocket-jingle I got left."

She stared up at him in awkward silence. He said, "You got to get right back and make sure nobody's jumped your claim, huh?"

She nodded soberly, and said, "Gordo does not think any of those claim jumpers made it and, even if any did, there is no way anyone can claim my poor papa's mine as long as I, his heredera, still draw breath. Pero some at the county seat may think I was killed along with all those others, so about that coach, and my need for an escort . . ."

He started to object she'd just said a fool army troop would be tagging along after her coach. Then he recalled how improper it was for a highborn Spanish gal, or even a Mexican chica, to traipse about on her own in public. So he said, "Well, I'll see you safe back to Deming if you'll pay both our fares. I ain't being Scotch. I'm just broke."

Considering how long it had taken Seth to get from Deming to Lordsburg the confusing way, the sixty-mile trip by Butterfield seemed astoundingly smooth and short. They rolled to a halt in front of the Deming coach stop just after sundown, and as the crowd turned out to admire the gallant if dusty troopers who'd followed them over the mountains without incident, nobody seemed to be paying attention as Seth helped Felicidad down from their coach.

The other four passengers had baggage to worry about. Seth helped Felicidad up to the plank walk in the tricky gloaming light, saying, "Well, here we are, and now all I got to do is see you to your door. You did say you'll be staying with that widowed aunt you mentioned for now, right?"

She nodded, and said, "Until I find out whether those Indians burned us out again up in the mountains. The one good thing about owning a gold mine is that you can always rebuild, as long as nobody takes the claim itself away from you."

He said that made sense, and when she said her aunt's place lay down that way, in the old Spanish Quarter, he gave her his good left elbow and they started walking, catching a few odd looks as they passed less dusty folk, with her packing that Winchester.

As they turned down down a narrow side street leading to the cottonwood-lined banks of the Rio Mimbres, she asked where he planned to stay until he could board that stage to Tombstone, as if it didn't matter to her at all. He shrugged, and said, "It's hard to plan that far ahead when you're strapped for jingle. But I'll manage, I always have."

She smiled softly, and said, "Forgive me. I had forgotten you were such an experienced world traveler. Pero it occurs to me my mine in the mountains is much closer than any in Tombstone could be, and you know I may have to rebuild from scratch."

He replied, "That's the best offer I've had since I headed west, Miss Felicidad. But what use would I be to you if I was dumb enough to take you up on it? I don't speak Spanish. If I did, I still wouldn't know beans about gold mining."

She asked what he meant to do out in Tombstone if that was the case. He answered simply, "Start at the bottom, if my uncle can get me a job to begin with. But at least I'll be working under a boss as speaks English.''

She said, ''I speak English, Seth.''

Before he could answer they both became aware of the two figures standing in the shade of a tree on the cinder path ahead. Felicidad murmured, ''Let me handle it. I am well known to those of my raza in this part of town.''

But as they got within conversational range of the two blocking their way, Seth blinked, and called out, ''Is that you, Wagner?''

Kid Wagner answered pleasantly enough. ''It wasn't easy. Me and Virgin Joe here just got in this afternoon after riding all over Robin Hood's Barn. Ran into old Ynez, that friendly gal Little Dipper was pals with, and she told us you'd made it out the back way to Lordsburg after all. How's your arm, Jersey Lilly? Heard Gus Hudson pinked it for you.''

Seth said, ''My fault. I passed on a chance to backshoot him. You boys have the advantage on me, no offense. I still don't know where the two of you were, or what you were doing, when all that lead commenced to fly back there.''

Virgin Joe laughed, and said, ''Old Elmo told us what was coming. Unlike yourself, we was too smart to tell him outright we meant to sit the dance out. But that's what we done, just the same.''

Kid Wagner added, ''He ain't telling the whole story. We didn't just stand aside. We ran for it, away from them blinky lights you set up, as soon as the fun and games commenced.''

Virgin Joe explained. ''Time we come back, it was all over. You-all had lit out but left us plenty of ponies and supplies nobody left in camp had any use for. The infernal, ah, Mexicans seemed to have got all the money on the boys they left scattered about. But figuring the Apache was chasing you, we cut back the way we'd come in in the first place, and so here we all are, and ain't that swell?''

Seth didn't answer. Kid Wagner said, ''What Joe's getting at is that you're a good old boy, and we're going to need even more like you if we're going to file on that abandoned gold mine now that poor old Elmo and even Gus and his crew are out of the picture. You see how it is, now, don't you?''

Seth certainly did, but Felicidad protested, ''Have you both lost your minds? Is true both my Tío Pablo and my father are dead, but what about *my* rights to the claim?''

Kid Wagner told her calmly, ''Greaser gals don't have no rights a white man don't see fit to give 'em, you pretty little thing.''

And then he was dead. For Seth Grant had been taught by the late Gus Hudson what could happen to a man who kept shooting off his mouth instead of shooting with serious intent, and it was still mighty close. For though he blew Virgin Joe through a cactus hedge with his second shot he'd have gone down with the both of them if Felicidad hadn't spun with her Winchester, firing from the hip to down the rascal drawing a bead on Seth's back.

As they stood there, shocked by their own survival and the ringing in their ears, Seth asked her, ''How did you know?''·

She said, ''Call me a tomboy. My people also let one or two do all the talking while the serious one circles around to jump the victim from the rear. Pero who *was* the third one, eh?''

Seth moved in on the one she'd downed, his six-gun in hand lest he be wrong about that limp sprawl. But he wasn't. He recognized the dead face from among those Gus Hudson had ridden in with, and told her, ''Your boys didn't get all of Hudson's guys after all. Do we really have to worry about the conversation the three of them had back at your claim once the smoke commenced to clear?''

She said they'd as much as confessed in detail, and asked, ''Do you think they really meant to cut you in, had you gone along with them?''

He shrugged and said they'd never know now. Not a window shade was moving up and down the narrow street, as far as Seth could see. But he wasn't too surprised when a familiar figure wearing a familiar badge hove into view, calling out, ''Whatever just transpired, this is the law coming in. So let's not nobody act silly, hear?''

They didn't. As the town law Seth had met before joined them he found Seth with his six-gun holstered and Felicidad aiming her carbine politely at the dirt. The somewhat blustersome old lawman ticked his hat brim, saying, ''Evening, Miss Robles. I see you seem to be alive and well, whilst three other gents lie all about like bear rugs. So is it safe to assume this homicidal lunatic here is on your side?''

Seth started to explain. The town law hushed him, and said, ''I was talking to the lady, Grant. I know you aim to say it was self-defense. I want to hear what the daughter of an old friend has to say about your latest shootout.''

Felicidad demurely told the lawman, ''Seth only got two. I had to shoot one. They were out to do me for my gold claim.''

The town law nodded grimly, and said, ''I heard there was a lot of that going on. Talked to your segundo, Gordo, earlier today.''

Turning at last to Seth, the old-timer said, ''All right, you done a good deed, you murderous young cuss. Only this time you're really going to have to satisfy the coroner's jury, and with the Fourth of July weekend coming up, Lord knows when they'll get around to it, and we have a vagrancy law in this county. So unless you can show some visible means of support, I don't rightly see how we'll be able to let you run loose that long."

Felicidad said, "Don't be silly, he has a job. We were just talking about it when these three claim jumpers tried to put me out of business."

The old-timer fixed Seth with a keen look, saying, "That right, boy? Seems last time we talked you said you were just passing through and didn't want no job in these parts."

Seth smiled sheepishly, glanced at Felicidad in the gathering dusk, and answered, "That was then. This is now. And anything beats spending the Fourth of July in jail."

About the Author

Lou Cameron created the "bible" for the popular *Long-arm* western series. In 1976 he won the Spur Award for *The Spirit Horses*. Cameron is also a writer of crime novels.

His latest westerns for Fawcett include *The Buntline Special* and *Crooked Lance*.

JIM MILLER'S
SHARP-SHOOTIN'
ST●RIES
O' THE WAYS
O' THE WEST!!